F ↙
you

D1236478

250
North Avenue

74
186

Guns of Darkness

Guns
of
Darkness

CARTER TRAVIS YOUNG

DOUBLEDAY & COMPANY, INC.

GARDEN CITY, NEW YORK

1974

All of the characters in this book
are fictitious and any resemblance
to actual persons, living or dead,
is purely coincidental.

Library of Congress Cataloging in Publication Data

Young, Carter Travis.
Guns of darkness.

I. Title.
PZ4.Y68Gu [PS3575.O7] 813'.5'4
ISBN 0-385-00320-X
Library of Congress Catalog Card Number 74–9147

First Edition

Copyright © 1974 by Doubleday & Company, Inc.

*This one is for
Sam Barker*

ONE

Viewed in the cool shadows of evening, it was a pretty town, sheltered by the scythelike sweep of hills to the north and west, its early sprinkling of lights an inviting glow against the deepening purple of the grassy plain stretching beyond it to the east. Behind the rider were the raw switchbacks of the Cove Mountains he had crossed, but here the foothills were softly sculpted all around, their clefts and curves as lovely and mysterious as a sleeping woman. If you let your fancy go, you could feel the warm, soft breeze like a breath against your cheek, and sense a slow rise and fall of rounded hills.

Owen Conagher smiled.

The flash of white teeth was vivid in the dusty, weathered tan of his face. It eased the sharp planes of features that might have seemed harsh to a casual glance, even cold. The nose was strongly bridged, the cheekbones as high and prominent as an Indian's, the chin long and stubborn. The man's mouth and eyes relieved that harshness, in the way spring flowers or greenery around a spring softened the bleak emptiness of the prairie. The mouth was wide and firm, but it lacked any mean or sullen pull, and there were lines at the corners suggesting a quirky humor. The deep-set brown eyes were steady and thoughtful, and the amusement lingered in them after his brief smile vanished, amusement directed as much upon himself as upon his fanciful imaginings.

He was a tall man, lean and hard as a rail. His clothes were faded and dusty without being shabby, the choice of a man who owned few things but selected what he had not for flash or show, but for comfort and serviceability over the long haul. In his dark blue shirt and sweat-darkened vest, he had appeared like a man in black to the eyes that had sighted him at a distance just before sundown. The fact had been remarked, along with the coloring of his rangy horse, a chestnut with a white blaze on his forehead whose coat had caught a red fire from the last rays of the sun behind him.

Unaware of that earlier scrutiny, Conagher started down the long grade, following a wagon trail that speared the town below, studying its clustered buildings with a casual but quickening interest as he approached.

The business district consisted of some two-score clapboard buildings facing each other across the single main street. Some optimist had laid out a formidable grid of parallel and cross streets to the north and south of this central artery, but many of the grids enclosed only a few scattered houses and some were disappearing behind tall grass and brush.

Still, the town seemed alive enough, and at this hour inviting. A creek wound out of the hills to the southwest, swung left in front of the town, and circled it before wandering off across the sage plain to the east. There was a narrow wooden bridge over the creek, and cottonwoods stood tall along its banks like a bulwark before the town.

Conagher wondered how many such towns he had looked down upon, how many had appeared as peaceful and inviting as this one at the end of a long, dusty ride.

Too many.

For an instant he felt a tug of melancholy, the feeling that will sometimes threaten to engulf a man who has spent too much of his time alone in empty wastes and high, solitary spaces, a man without roots, without attachments, without any piece of earth to call his own, with none of the permanent ties that hobbled most men in one narrow place. Conagher was such a wanderer, restless, questing, resisting strong attachments because they threatened something vital in him—that very need to be unfettered, dependent on no one, free as the wind.

But surely the time would come when he wouldn't be quite so curious about what lay beyond the next ridge. Conagher recognized this and wondered if the urge to find his own place wasn't growing a mite stronger with enough years in his bones to make them hold their aches longer.

He hadn't found anything strong enough to hold him. That's what it came down to.

Did the little town of Bitter Creek hold such a reason? Its twilight appeal could be deceptive.

Too many towns, he thought again. Too many to yield to passing tugs of sentiment or yearning. Experience had bred caution, a hard-won skepticism about the welcoming aspects of such prairie towns. Too often they housed as many withered hopes as optimistic dreams, as much suspicion as welcome for a stranger riding in, as many bitter or warring factions as friendly neighbors. Even the name of the place gave pause: Bitter Creek. Why bitter? Because of the taste of its water? Or the blood spilled in it?

Always, coming to a strange place, there was curiosity and expectation, the wonder if this might be the town he had always been searching for, the one that would tempt him at last to settle down—not in the town itself, for he could never be that confined, but on a piece of land not far away, where the restless urge that had always kept him moving on would grow quiet. His skepticism, Conagher recognized, was an instinctive defense against this question. The fiddle foot in him was quick to discourage any such thoughts of lighting long enough in one place for roots to grow.

With a wry shrug of his wide shoulders, Conagher banished the speculation. Curiosity remained.

The town was more than peaceful. It was unnaturally still. There were no children calling shrilly at play after supper along the banks of the creek. Perhaps a dozen horses were tied along the rails of the main street, and a few wagons were pulled up here and there, but there was hardly any noise or movement. Maybe the whole town was at a meeting, Conagher thought, or in church for evening services. Was it Saturday or Sunday? He lost track of days along the trail, and he wasn't sure.

And it was not a sick town, one of those half-abandoned places, dying slowly because the railroad had passed it by or drought had sucked all the juices from it. Bitter Creek looked healthy enough, its buildings in good repair, a few new houses to balance the nondescript shacks clinging to the edges, a white painted church, a main street with board-walks swept cleaner than most. What ailed her, then?

Something nagged at Owen Conagher's memory a moment before he could capture it. While he groped in his mind, Big Red clopped over the wooden bridge past the sentinel cottonwoods that lined the creek. Conagher's gaze was diverted toward one tall tree that stood a little apart from two others of similar size. What caught his eye was a high, sturdy branch that seemed in the thickening darkness to have a smooth, worn spot. A hanging tree. Well, every town had need of one, just as it needed a Boot Hill. Conagher returned to the puzzling sense of something familiar. He felt Big Red's pace quicken as the rangy horse sensed the immediate meaning of this town for him— water and feed and rest at the end of a long ride. As if by instinct, Red swung right rather than heading along the main street, pointing his nose toward the livery stables. Conagher, still puzzling, gave him his head.

Then it came to him. A New Mexico town, peaceful and pretty like this one, but with a stillness that held a peculiar tension. Conagher had ridden into San Tomaso and smack into the middle of a range war. The town's

main street had been a battle line, with the two warring
factions holed up on either side, waiting for the other to
make a move. The silence of that town had been the breath-
caught quiet of waiting, the stillness of death.

Was Bitter Creek a battleground?

Short of the livery stables, identified by a wind-scrubbed,
painted sign that read WHITEY SMITH'S CORRAL,
Owen Conagher pulled up. He sat for a moment, listening.
His nostrils flared like an animal's, as if he sought the
very smell of danger. Beneath him Big Red stirred restlessly and gave his head a little, impatient toss. "In a minute, son," Conagher murmured. "Take it easy."

Somewhere up the street, a door opened and light pud-
dled the alleyway behind one of the store buildings. Conagher heard a man's voice and then, clearly, a woman's
laughter.

He relaxed. There had been no laughter in San Tomaso
that day. And, now that he thought about it, the rivals had
made themselves visible enough, peering from behind
their shades and windows and barricades, so that everyone knew something was up, and a stranger knew that he
had to choose one side of the street or light a shuck for
other parts. And no one had left his horse tied to a rail in
the line of fire.

With a shrug, Conagher let the big chestnut go, heading
toward the corral. This end of the town was mostly in
darkness except for the pool of light from a lantern hung
next to the open doors of the livery stables. As Conagher
neared the barn, he saw another wavering light moving
around inside, throwing huge shadows that created grotesque shapes within. Whitey Smith was coming, sensing
business where Conagher had sensed danger.

Maybe that was what he disliked about towns, Conagher
thought; he felt safer among the natural hazards of the
open, be they lightning or flood or angry varmint. They
might surprise you sometimes, but mostly they were pre-

dictable. Even a rattler was fairly predictable in his habits, and he always gave warning before he struck. Not so an angry or frightened man.

A bowlegged old-timer followed the wavering shadows thrown by his lantern into the doorway, peering toward Conagher as he crossed the yard. The old man raised his light high and squinted, blinking moist eyes. The light shone off his pink scalp, around which a halo of thinning white hair fell limply. Maybe he was like that old Greek, Diogenes, looking for an honest man. *Not this time, old man*, Conagher thought. *I've bent the truth some in my time, though I'd say I was as straight as most, and straighter than some.*

Whitey Smith stepped forward a few paces. "Evenin', stranger," he called out in a quavery voice.

"Howdy. Got room for a hungry horse?"

"Sure enough," the little man said quickly. He set his lantern on a smooth-topped stump well away from the stable doors. As Conagher reined in, the owner of the corral shuffled back a step. "Plenty room. You jist bring him on in."

Funny, Conagher thought. Afterward he knew that he had heard nervous fear in the white-haired old man's words, just as he had sensed something amiss in the way Whitey set his lantern down so carefully and retreated. But in that moment there was no time to reason anything out. Any curiosity in Conager's mind about Whitey Smith was banished by the abrupt return of a strong feeling of danger. It was sharp, palpable. Danger quivered in the night's stillness. It was something he could smell and feel, as sharp as the sweat of fear.

Conagher was near the open doors to the stables, silhouetted there clearly, caught in the overlapping pools of light thrown out by the two lanterns, which cast the surrounding shadows into deeper blackness. He was a sitting duck, Conagher thought.

A target.

The reality of the threat struck with the painful force of a blow in the small of the back. The little stable owner chose that moment to scuttle around the corner of the entrance and dive for cover. In the same instant, Conagher moved.

Then all hell broke loose.

TWO

The crash of gunfire cut into Bud Selvy's laughter. For an instant his good-natured face hardened into a cold, dangerous stillness, offering a fleeting glimpse of something quite different from the image he generally presented. Willa Colgrove caught that momentary change and felt a shock of wonder.

Then Selvy smiled again. "Sounds like the Reception Committee is receiving," he said.

"Then he's come. The man who's . . . after you."

"Sounds like it unless I missed out on my dates somewhere and this is the Fourth of July."

"Don't joke about it. It's not a laughing matter."

"Not for him, I reckon," Selvy answered with irrepressible humor.

"Not for your committee neither," Dan Colgrove said from his rocking chair in the shadows at the far end of the porch. "It's dirty work for good men." Pointedly he added, "Your dirty work, Selvy."

Selvy swung to face him, staring at the older man's lean, bent shadow. "It wasn't my idea, this committee. You know that, Dan."

"Way I heard it, it was supposed to be Dick Sanderson's idea. That would make it Dick's first original idea since he run out on that family of his back in Kansas."

"Pa, that's not fair!"

Bud Selvy chuckled amiably. "I expect that's true enough about Sanderson. It was Ike Coolidge who grabbed the reins if you want the truth of it. But that's of no account. I didn't like the whole thing any better than you, sir. I tried to talk 'em out of it, and that's a fact. They wouldn't listen to me."

"That must have been a rare experience for you then."

"Stop sniping at Mr. Selvy, Pa," Willa Colgrove said, this time more sharply.

"I wasn't doing the serious sniping," her father answered. "That come from the other side of town."

But he sounded subdued by Willa's warning, and there was a moment's silence on the front porch of the frame house. All three people there listened for more shooting, but after the initial burst of fire, there was only stillness. Willa wondered what that quiet meant. Had the gunman approaching Bitter Creek on his murderous quest been cut down so quickly? Was the threat he had posed to Bud Selvy ended so easily? And if that was so, if the danger was over, why did she remain so unsettled, so uneasy in her mind? Why was there no real relief, no sudden joy?

Restless, Willa turned away from Selvy, wandering along the porch to the front steps, which faced north toward the business district a short distance away. The movement brought her into the light falling across the porch from the open doorway. A stranger watching from nearby might have been surprised, for the figure etched by the light was as tall as an average man's. In fact Willa Colgrove stood six inches over five feet tall in her bare feet, and she looked down on many men. Even in his boots Bud Selvy had to pull himself erect to be at eye level with her—one reason she had taken to wearing moccasins, as she did now, or low-heeled shoes when she worked in the office of Selvy's Freight Line.

She had on the same long skirt and puff-sleeved blouse she had been wearing that afternoon when Ralph Reese, the town's part-time deputy and only representative of law when Sheriff Crowder was away, burst into the office with the news that the stranger had been sighted coming down from Cove Pass. Bud Selvy had abruptly sent Willa home. She had been too nervous to change clothes for the evening and hadn't even thought of them until Selvy unexpectedly appeared at the house shortly after dark. She was not conscious of them now, nor of the appearance she presented to the two men on the porch with her as she paused in the panel of light before the door. The line of the skirt combined with her height to make her seem slimmer than she was. A closer look revealed the promise of generous fullness beneath the starched shirt and the straight, plain skirt. She was a striking young woman, drawing an appreciative stare from Selvy even at this moment of tense waiting. Worry had shaded her eyes, and in the dimness the hint of strange color in them—a kind of violet or lavender—was not visible. But the pride was evident in her stance, the clean fineness of feature, the soft, full lips, the richness of thick, dark hair imprisoned in braids and piled somehow behind her head because she despised her dense tangle of impossible curls, the strength of will that made her a formidable match for any man. And a tempting prize, Selvy thought.

At the age of twenty-three, Willa Colgrove joked about being too old to interest a man, but the threat of spinsterhood did not truly alarm her. She was single, she believed, in part because her height had frightened smaller men away but more because she had developed early in life a chronic inability to play the helpless, dumb creature expected of her. Often on her own when her father was operating the freight line before his accident, she had grown up independent, running a household from the age of twelve when her mother died, learning to handle her father's accounts in the office almost as soon. She had not been a helpless girl yearning to find shelter under a man's protective arm, and in truth no man had seriously interested her before Bud Selvy came to Bitter Creek.

That had been two years ago. He had purchased the

mercantile from Howie Stenholm. Then, a year later, when Dan Colgrove was left crippled after the crash of a runaway wagon whose brakes had failed to hold, Bud Selvy had stepped in and purchased the line, paying cash. He had disclaimed any charitable impulse, insisting that the move was good business, but Willa knew there were many in town who believed that Selvy had paid too high a price at a time when Dan Colgrove stood to lose the business by default. Selvy had been eager for Willa to stay on at the office as before and Willa had also heard the rumors hinting that she was the principal reason for Selvy's generosity.

Bud Selvy seemed to be the kind of man who inspired rumors. He was talked about, for one thing. Everyone liked him for his easy humor. And he was demonstrably a man to watch, a man who knew how to make things go his way, a man with a future. One whisper said that he had lent Dick Sanderson money and was now a silent partner in Sanderson's Feed & Grain. Another found links between his success and the prosperity of Ike Coolidge's Cattleman's Bank. And still another—which Willa knew to be true—concerned his recent purchase of a large section of land next to Tug Walsh's spread south of town, with the thought of raising cattle and eventually building a home there.

None of these factors accounted for the fact that Willa Colgrove had been on the verge of accepting Bud Selvy's repeated proposals at last. He had interested her initially by being the first man in many years to show no awe of her, the first ever to laugh off her occasional displays of temper —flare-ups which she did not fully understand herself. He was also the only man who had managed to make her feel a little unsure of herself, and thus held her interest.

Was that what bothered her now? She had shrugged off her father's criticism of Bud Selvy's role in the forming of the Reception Committee. She knew that Dan Colgrove disliked Selvy. Beyond a fatherly reluctance to admit that any man was good enough for her, there was the fact that

Dan had never got over a lingering, wholly natural resentment of the way Selvy had taken over his business and made a much bigger success of it than Dan ever had, while he was relegated to rocking chair and walking stick. But had his scornful sniping found a sore spot in her?

Wasn't it up to a man to fight his own fights, even if they threatened to be dangerous, rather than letting his friends do it for him?

Bud Selvy stepped closer to her, as if he sensed the remoteness in her and the worry behind it. Standing beside her near the steps, his figure loomed bulky in contrast to her slender height. Although he was not tall, he was a powerfully built man, with big shoulders and arms, wide hips, thighs like great hams. That suggestion of physical power frightened her a little, and in dark night hours of wonder she attributed the reaction to a spinster's suppressed desires—a conclusion of which she remained uncertain.

Willa found Selvy's appearance pleasing, if not outright handsome. He had sandy hair, snapping blue eyes, and somewhat pudgy features. The outlines of rounded cheeks and chin and fleshy nose were slightly blurred, as if they had been formed by hand out of soft dough or clay instead of being sharply chiseled from harder substance. The effect was pleasing, perhaps, because his was such a sunny face, the blue eyes always teasing or twinkling with humor, the mouth smiling so often that it seemed almost never to be at rest.

Her father held even this against him, she thought ruefully. He called Bud Selvy, with biting accuracy that held a trace of contempt, the Laughing Man.

"What are you thinking, hon?" Selvy asked quietly.

"About him," she said evasively. "That gunfighter. What kind of man he is." *Or was,* she thought.

"Not the kind for you to fret over."

"But what kind—"

"What does it matter?"

She turned to face him. "It does matter, Bud. You know it does. Maybe only because he came here after you, but that's reason enough."

"He's a killer," Selvy said shortly. "There's no scarcity of such men in this country, Willa, even if you haven't known them. Be glad you haven't. They're men who like hurting and killing, who take pride in it. Some do it for money, some for pure pleasure. This one . . . well, he hired out for it, so I guess that says it plain enough. They're the worst kind." When Willa shivered, he placed a hand on her arm and kept it there. She made no attempt to remove it, but she was surprised that the idea even occurred to her. "I know what you've been thinking, you and your father. That a man should handle his own quarrels. But I have no quarrel with this gunslinger, and that's a fact. The man I quarreled with is long dead. I'm sorry for that, but it can't be changed. It's his family that still want their pound of flesh—an eye for an eye, my life for his. But they haven't the guts to come after me themselves. They hired a gunman for it, a stranger to me, so maybe it's only justice that strangers cut that stranger down. It isn't what I wanted. Damn it, I never asked for help, you know that. But you heard Coolidge and Sanderson and the others. They wanted me kept out of this, and they brought Reese into the committee to make everything legal so no charge could be made against me."

Willa Colgrove was silent. Everything Selvy said was plausible, reasonable, sensible. She could even accept it in her mind. And yet . . .

"I guess I'd better get into my hole at the Dust Cutter until I know what's happened," Selvy said, and now there was a trace of bitterness in his tone that touched her. She wanted to protest it, but the words failed to come.

"Yes, I expect you'd better get down there," Dan Colgrove said from his chair in the shadows. "It's quiet now."

Bud Selvy released Willa's arm, and she sensed a sudden concentration of force in him as he swung to stare at her father. But instead of making an angry retort, Selvy unexpectedly chuckled. "You're bein' ornery tonight, Dan. Damned if I don't think you wanted to see me go up alone against that hardcase just so's you'd get your business back."

"Now, see here—"

But the younger man laughed, and in so doing easily turned Dan Colgrove's wrath aside. "You can't get rid of me that easily. Anyway"—he glanced back at Willa with a twinkle in his eyes—"I'm all for keeping the business in the family. All Willa has to do is say the word."

Selvy allowed her only an instant to react, his gaze holding hers. Then he started down the steps. "Stay inside," he said over his shoulder. "I'll let you know—"

Two quick shots broke off his comment. Willa Colgrove flinched with each new explosion.

Bud Selvy stopped in his tracks, one foot on the bottom step. He stared off toward the far end of town, the direction from which the shots had come, and Willa regretted not being able to see his face.

As new silence lengthened, Willa asked, "What does it mean, Bud?"

"It means he's alive," Selvy answered, and there was a harshness in his voice she had not heard before.

"They missed him," Dan Colgrove said. "Ain't one of them town wolves can shoot worth a lick, exceptin' Reese when he's sober. And Tug Walsh, who ain't a townman at all. Walsh must have missed."

Bud Selvy turned upon him with sudden, unwonted viciousness. "Then maybe you'll get your wish! Maybe you'll see me put under."

"Bud, he didn't mean—"

"Take him inside," Selvy said curtly. His tone abruptly softened. "And stay there with him until this is over. Maybe he was right all along. I know it was in your mind, too. That this is my fight. Well, it is now. It won't help if I'm worrying about you."

"We can take care of ourselves!" Dan Colgove snapped, a grievance in his tone, as if he had not expected his caustic comments to be taken seriously or turned against him.

Selvy surprised Willa again by chuckling. "I expect you can, Dan. They should've had you on the committee."

"You don't know for certain the man's escaped," Willa said, surprised by the sharpness of her concern now that the danger was not something just talked about but as blunt and real as the crash of gunshots close by.

"Don't know anything for certain," Selvy answered, "except that I want you both out of the way and safe."

He moved away from the steps, melting almost instantly into deep shadows. As soon as he was lost to sight, Willa Colgrove felt panic leap into her throat. "Bud, we're wrong!" she cried. "Let the law handle it—the committee . . ."

From the darkness Selvy's answer drifted to her. "There'll be no law in Bitter Creek tonight exceptin' the law that gunslick brought with him, and that comes from the end of a gun or a rope!"

"There are enough of them on the committee," she heard herself plead with a kind of desperation. "And Sheriff Crowder will be back soon. You can stay out of it. Bud? Are you there?"

Around her the night was still. As she listened tensely, all she could hear was the heavy thudding of her own heartbeat.

THREE

"I hit the blighter!" Alfred Williams cried from the hay-loft overlooking the entrance to the stables. "I tell you, I hit him!"

"He's in the barn," Ike Coolidge yelled. "Don't let him out—we've got him boxed in!"

From his postion across the yard, facing the open door-way through which the stranger had abruptly disappeared, Tug Walsh swore softly. If those damned fools kept up their yelping, they would get themselves all killed. And maybe him along with them.

Which just might happen anyway, he thought sourly.

Walsh felt a sense of the absurdity of his position, lying prone on his belly inside the spring wagon he had brought into town that afternoon for supplies. The smoking barrel of his cedar-handled Colt was inches from his face as he peered through a crack between two boards of the wagon, sighting across the yard toward the stables. He wished that he hadn't chanced to leave his rifle that very day at the gunsmith's for repairs, the new stock he had ordered being ready to install. He would have given a lot to have had his rifle in his hands when the stranger rode in and the shooting started.

Tug Walsh wished, in fact, that he had chosen another day entirely to ride into town. He was a last-minute addition to this Reception Committee, having been recruited that afternoon. He hadn't seen a way to turn down so impressive a group of the town's leading citizens—impressive, that is, when you met them on their own grounds, in their stores and offices. Not here at Whitey Smith's Corral, where Walsh could certainly have chosen a fitter crew for a deadly ambush.

A cattleman who had fought for everything he had, Tug Walsh had been through his share of scrapes, and he didn't shrink from another. But there were aspects about this one that bothered him, not least of which were the nervous trigger fingers of his partners. Six men with a clear shot at a single target, and they hadn't brought him down. Walsh was certain the rider on the chestnut had been hit, although he put no faith in his own late and hasty shot. But the man had smelled danger and reacted swiftly. He was already diving from his horse before the first shot crashed, and he had vanished into the darkness of the stables in a mighty big hurry for someone badly hurt.

Walsh tried to place each of his companions, the members of the Reception Committee, wondering if the silent killer in the barn was doing the same.

The only one Walsh could see clearly was Isiah Howarth, stationed with his carbine behind the horse trough along the south side of the yard, not far from Walsh's wagon. Howarth was the editor of the Bitter Valley *Gazette*. A bristling, feisty, independent man, but a man of words rather than guns. It was a surprise to find him lined up in a vigilante group, but Walsh guessed that that was a tribute to Bud Selvy.

Dick Sanderson, proprietor of Sanderson's Feed & Grain, was in one of the box stalls inside the stables, a position Walsh did not envy him at the moment. Sanderson, like Walsh, was armed only with a six-shooter. Sanderson could handle a gun well enough, Walsh judged, but his nerve was a more open question.

On the far side of the yard, flanking Walsh's wagon in order to catch the intended victim of the ambush in a tri-angulated crossfire, was Ralph Reese, the deputy. Reese was also relief man at the hotel. The part-time deputy was not much of a substitute for Ed Crowder when you came right down to the hard of it. Walsh knew Reese as an expert drink cadger with a hollow leg and a tendency to turn whisky-mean. Still, he was big and tough as well as mean, no one to fool with in a fight. Tug Walsh had placed more confidence in Reese's Winchester over there behind the woodpile than in any of the other weapons brought to bear on the stranger as he rode in. If the rider had been hit before he spilled off his chestnut, Walsh guessed that it would be a bullet from Reese's Winchester he carried in him.

The remaining two members of the Reception Committee had placed themselves clearly—and foolishly—with their yelling. One was the little Englishman, Alfred Williams, a pharmacist who had opened his shop that spring and was anxious to prove himself one of Bitter Creek's finest. Walsh envied him two things: his position in the loft and his superb English Manton rifle, beautifully finished and engraved. It hadn't enabled Williams to shoot accurately— his had been the easiest shot at the mounted gunman directly in front of the loft window—but Walsh attributed that to excitement and inexperience, not to the fine weapon. The final member of the vigilantes, and the most vocal spokesman who had talked Tug Walsh into joining them, was Ike Coolidge, crouching somewhere in the deep shadows at the southeast corner of the barn, armed with a shotgun. How in hell Coolidge had managed to miss everything at such close range with a wide spread of shot was beyond Walsh, except that Ike Coolidge belonged in his bank counting money with his deft, soft hands, not here in the darkness of an ambuscade.

Six men, and there was no absolute certainty that their intended victim had been wounded seriously. Just before the man disappeared, Walsh had had an impression that he stumbled, as if jolted by the impact of a bullet. But even that was little more than a hunch. It didn't mean the trouble was over. It meant the real trouble was only beginning.

"Damn!" Walsh swore again under his breath, his thoughts playing over the frantic moment of the shooting. If only that Englishman hadn't been too eager and high with his shot . . . or if Coolidge had been able to hit the side of a barn with his shotgun . . . or if Ralph Reese hadn't had a bottle over there with him behind the woodpile . . . or . . .

But there were too many ifs. And they all went back to the first one: If Dick Sanderson hadn't had the luck to hear about the gunman over in Colton earlier that week, a stranger named Rorke who was asking about someone who shaped up like Bud Selvy, there would have been no Reception Committee at all, and Tug Walsh wouldn't have found himself lying in the wagon bed in the darkness, chilled and sweating at the same time, knowing that in a few minutes he might have to go into that barn after the wounded man, knowing that it would be like crawling into a cave after an angry bear. . . .

Dick Sanderson had been closing an order for three wagonloads of oats in Colton when he heard about the stranger from Burt Angstrom, who was selling him the grain. Sanderson had signed the order and Angstrom was placing it in his desk when he glanced up quizzically. "I reckon things are lookin' up for you now, Sanderson."

"I'm not complainin'."

"I mean, since you and that Selvy feller become partners."

"Where'd you hear that?"

"Well, it's what I heard around."

"Well, you heard wrong. I know Bud Selvy, sure, and you can bet he's a good friend in a pinch—he's helped me out some. But partners? No sirree."

"I guess I heard wrong then."

"I reckon you did."

Angstrom closed the desk drawer with a slap. Rising, he came through the counter gate. "My treat," he said, acknowledging their ritual of a drink to seal a deal in the Happy Days saloon across the street. At the door Angstrom stopped short and Sanderson nearly blundered into him. Angstrom looked up—he was a short, potbellied man with quick, sly eyes that had a way of losing themselves behind their folds of flesh when he was haggling over a bargain or holding a hand of cards—and Sanderson saw speculation and a decision in those quick eyes. "Reason I brought it up, about Selvy, there's a feller hangin' around town, calls himself Rorke. He's lookin' for somebody. Man he's askin' about carries a different name—Niles Asher or somethin' close—but I'd swear the way he describes Asher he's a dead ringer for that Selvy."

Sanderson shrugged. He was dry and ready to dismiss vague gossip. "That so? I don't see why . . ."

He paused then. Burt Angstrom wasn't given to idle talk. He seemed always to be too busy making money to have time for it. Sanderson studied him more closely.

"Who is this man—the one askin' questions? A lawman? That it?"

Angstrom shook his head. "That's the thing, Dick. He don't wear a badge. He just goes around soft and quiet, askin' his questions, playin' a little monte over at the Happy Days and keepin' his ears pricked. And there's somethin' else: He wears his guns tied down real low in a couple of those greased Mexican loop holsters, one for each side. You get the feeling either one of them guns is gonna jump out into his hand if he wants it to. Unless I miss my guess, that man's a gunman, Dick. And he's mighty inquisitive about somebody who resembles your partner, who might've come through this way a couple years back." Angstrom paused. "Ain't that when Selvy came along?"

This time Sanderson did not think to deny the silent partnership Angstrom alluded to, a fact that had somehow found its way in rumor across the Cove Mountains separating Colton from Bitter Creek. His mind was racing too quickly, dredging up curiosity and concern and then anxiety.

Anxiety quickly dominated his feelings. If there was any threat to Bud Selvy in the offing—and that was what Burt Angstrom was broadly hinting—Dick Sanderson was also threatened.

Sanderson was not a man who handled trouble well. Although still in his thirties, he had already held a score of jobs at one time or another and had seen three business enterprises of his own fail. When financial troubles and the unexpected discovery of an out-of-wedlock pregnancy had threatened an already shaky marriage, Sanderson had also deserted his wife and two children some eight years before in Kansas. He was not without a native shrewdness that had always enabled him somehow or other to bounce back from disaster and start over, and he could be a vicious fighter when backed to the wall. His weakness was of another kind. He had learned to expect trouble and failure; whenever things piled up on him, his first impulse was simply to run out.

The pattern had repeated itself in Bitter Greek. Bad judgment and what he regarded as a run of bad luck had pushed his feed and grain business to the edge of failure. This time, when Sanderson was beginning to panic, his good friend Bud Selvy had stepped in to shore up his courage. Selvy's loan, advice, and help had come at a high cost: 51 per cent of the business. Unaccountably, however, Selvy had seemed happy to remain a silent partner, allowing Sanderson to salvage his pride and reputation for the time being. The partnership had worked out to the satisfaction of both men. Sanderson even functioned better when the burdens of ultimate responsibility and decision making were not his.

But Sanderson knew in his heart that if something happened to Selvy, he would also go under.

Sanderson hung around Colton long enough that day to have the gunman pointed out to him. Angstrom's description had not been exaggerated. There was no doubt whatever in Sanderson's mind that Rorke was gunwise and bad medicine all the way. It was more than the man's cat-eyed look or the way he wore his twin six-guns low in their loop holsters. There was something wild and furious in Rorke that seemed to be on a very tight rein. You couldn't pass near him without feeling it. Once Rorke looked up and caught Sanderson staring at him. His cold, dead eyes seemed to look right past Sanderson's defenses. Sanderson felt as if his mind were stripped naked.

An hour later, shaken, Sanderson was on the stage bound for Bitter Creek. By then he was certain that Rorke was making inquiries about *him*. Sanderson was convinced that Rorke had perceived his fear and would probe the reason for it. He would soon learn who Sanderson was and where he hailed from.

The long stage ride, broken by a stopover at Ike Higgins's Summit Lodge at the opening of Long Neck Pass, quieted Sanderson's anxiety. He began to tell himself that he had been too quick to panic. What possible reason could a gunman—a hired killer, according to one story Sanderson had heard in Colton—have for tracking good-natured Bud Selvy? Surely the man he was hunting was someone else, someone who merely resembled Selvy. Moreover, Sanderson had not talked to Rorke, nor had he made any obvious blunder. The notion that he had betrayed his alarm in a moment's glance was foolishness. When he told his partner the story, Sanderson became convinced, Selvy would laugh at him.

But Selvy didn't laugh.

The stage reached Bitter Creek early in the morning after the downhill run. Sanderson found Selvy already at his office overlooking the corral and wagon yard of the freight line on the north side of town. Selvy, for all his happy-go-lucky ways, always seemed to be up and about earlier than anyone else. A dozen times Sanderson had promised himself that one of these days he would rise while it was still dark and offer Selvy a cheerful greeting from his own office window as Selvy passed by on the way to work. So far he hadn't managed it. Selvy was always ahead of him.

Sanderson accepted a cup of coffee and chuckled a little as he told his story of the inquisitive gunslinger in Colton. When he finished, he looked up expectantly, waiting for Selvy's answering laugh. Instead he was jolted by what he saw. Bud Selvy had turned maggot white. For an instant his jowls sagged and he appeared as if he might be sick on the spot. He rose so abruptly that his swivel chair skidded backward and crashed against the wall behind his desk.

"What is it, Mr. Selvy?" Sanderson asked in agitation. "You look . . ."

Selvy didn't seem to hear him. For a minute he stood rooted, his big hands opening and closing. Without warning, a bellow of rage erupted from his throat. He turned and grabbed his chair. Picking it up as if it were made of light kindling instead of heavy oak, he hurled it across the office. One leg caught an edge of the window as the chair smashed against the wall. Glass shattered explosively.

Willa Colgrove came running in from the outer office. "What happened? Mr. Selvy, what's wrong?"

She stared at him in amazement. Sanderson was also on his feet, astonishment causing him to gape with his mouth open. It was the first time he had ever seen Bud Selvy lose his composure, much less erupt in blind fury.

Selvy shook himself visibly, like a dog shaking off water. Simultaneously he seemed to become aware of Sanderson and of the girl who had burst into the office. Reason swam into his pale eyes like a silvery trout surfacing to the light.

In an instant it was hard to believe what had happened except for the evidence of broken glass on the floor and the chair lying on its side, one arm broken and the leading edge of the seat bearing a fresh white scar.

"It's nothing, Willa," he said quickly. "I told you I had a temper, didn't I? You'll have to tell your pa I'm not always the Laughing Man, after all."

"But—" She glanced at Sanderson, bewildered. "Is something wrong?"

"Nothin' we can't handle. Right, Dick?"

"Huh? Oh, uh, sure, Mr. Selvy. Sure."

Selvy talked Willa Colgrove out of the office. By the time he had the door closed behind her and turned back to Sanderson, he was himself again. He even managed a chuckle as he said, "Gave you a turn there, didn't I, Dick?" But there was a sober flatness in his eyes in place of the familiar twinkle.

"You must know this Rorke," Sanderson said tentatively. "That's it, ain't it, Mr. Selvy?"

"He sounds like somebody I knew once. Yeah, I know him."

"Then . . . it's you he's lookin' for?"

"Could be me. Yes, I'd say it's a damned strong possibility he's been trackin' me down."

"Why? Hell, Mr. Selvy, he's a killer! What does he want with you?"

"Well, now, that's plain enough, isn't it, Dick?" Selvy retrieved his chair, inspected it, and steered it back behind his desk. One caster rolled over a shard of glass with a crunch. Selvy tested the chair with one hand. His glance met Sanderson's and he smiled. "You said it yourself. He's comin' to kill me."

That curious scene between Sanderson and Selvy occurred Wednesday morning. The same afternoon a group of Bud Selvy's friends gathered with him in the office off the balcony of Selvy's Mercantile. In the two years since he had purchased Howie Stenholm's store, Selvy had made many friends among Bitter Creek's influential citizens as well as with his customers. His unflagging humor made him easy to like. His fair pricing, honest dealing, and capacity for hard work won respect. His visible success added something else. In a man less likable, it might have earned him envy and resentment, but Bud Selvy had been successful without making enemies. On the contrary, the other businessmen of Bitter Creek, some of whom might have been considered rivals, were eager to be known as his friends. They saw a man going places, concerned about the town's growth and prosperity as well as his own, a man whose success might rub off on those close to him as well as upon the town itself.

As a result, three of the men who answered his summons that day were members of the town council, and a fourth was working hard at becoming one. The members included Sanderson; Ike Coolidge, owner of the Cattleman's Bank; and Isiah Howarth, the owner of the town's only press and editor of the Bitter Valley *Gazette*. The fourth man, Alfred Williams, the druggist, had begun courting Bud Selvy's favor before he had been in Bitter Creek a month. Selvy had recently recommended Williams for membership on the council.

Bud Selvy produced a bottle before telling the men, each of whom was openly curious about the purpose of the meeting, what he had called them together for. He waited for the bottle to be passed around and returned to his desk before he poured two fingers into his own glass and surveyed the group.

"Gentlemen," he said finally, "I suppose you're all as curious as a virgin on her wedding night. All except my friend Dick, here, who has a pretty good notion what this is all about."

"You going to announce for Senator, Bud?" Ike Coolidge asked with a smile.

Selvy's own smile faded. He seemed to look inward for a moment, his expression sobering, before he replied. "Nothin' like that, Ike. But I like to think maybe you could have meant that seriously, or at least you wasn't makin' fun of me."

"You know better than that, Bud." Coolidge was one of the few who generally called Selvy by his first name. Not that Selvy demanded formality; the reverse was true. But most men held him in a little awe.

Selvy sighed. "I'll put it right out between the horns. You're all good friends of mine or you wouldn't be here. That's why I wanted you to hear this first, and I wanted you to have first crack at me. I'll be puttin' the Mercantile up for sale, and some other things as well. I'm pullin' out of Bitter Creek."

There was consternation in the crowded office. Surprise turned quickly to vocal protest. Isiah Howarth declared the town needed him. Williams pleaded with him to say that he was only joking. Dick Sanderson sat chilled and silent with his knowledge of the morning's explosion over his news. Finally Ike Coolidge, even more aghast than the others over the announcement, demanded to know in God's name why Selvy would leave what he had worked so hard to build up?

Selvy glanced at Sanderson as he waited for the group to quiet down. He took a long swallow, emptying his glass, and refilled it deliberately. He pushed the bottle across the desk, indicating that the others should refill their glasses. Sanderson poured his drink with a shaking hand.

"It's a long story, gentlemen, and I don't mind tellin' you that it's not one I relish sharing with you. But I reckon I owe you that much."

Then Selvy told them about Sanderson's trip to Colton and his discovery of the gunman whose inquiries seemed directed at finding Selvy. He drew a startled exclamation from Coolidge when he confessed that his real name was not Selvy but Niles Asher, and that he had come to Texas from Wyoming, not from Kansas as he had previously claimed. He was not, Selvy was quick to add, an outlaw or in any way a wanted man. But he was a hunted man—and Rorke was the hunter.

He had called himself by other names for more than three years, dating from a bitter quarrel with another man over a woman. The rival's name was Bascomb. He was one of two sons of a powerful Wyoming rancher. Orville Bascomb had always had things his own way simply because he was a Bascomb, and when he fell crazy in love with a young woman, he didn't expect anyone to stand in his way. The trouble was the girl seemed to like Selvy better, and the fact that Selvy didn't go after her just seemed to make her more eager to give herself to him.

The upshot was that Orville Bascomb forced a showdown with Selvy over the girl. Orville fancied himself a good hand with a gun, but he wasn't quite as sudden as he thought he was. Selvy received a flesh wound in the arm. His answering shot struck Bascomb in the heart.

At first Selvy had panicked and run. Then, when he learned that the law viewed the killing as a fair fight, concluding that Selvy had acted in self-defense, he was tempted to stay. Acting against that decision was the fact that the Bascombs refused to let the matter rest. Orville's brother, Billy, let it be known that he would draw on Selvy the first time they met, and Selvy knew that after Billy there would be the father, and after him an uncle and a couple of cousins. He could stay and fight it out with all of them until he was sick of killing, or he could run, no matter how much that went against his grain.

So he left Wyoming, took a new name, and tried to start a new life for himself in Colorado. A year later he was tracked there by the man named Rorke, a hired gunman with a formidable reputation in the high country. For a second time Selvy was forced to flee, knowing that after Rorke there would be others if he survived a shoot-out. His only hope was to find some place where he wouldn't be tracked down, to build a life free of violence and the enduring hatred of the Bascombs.

That hope had brought him to Bitter Creek, where he had given himself the name of Selvy. Now the hope was shattered once more. It was only a matter of days, perhaps hours, before Rorke came to seek him out.

For a while there was stunned silence after Bud Selvy finished his tale. At last Ike Coolidge spoke. "You've got to stop running sometime, Bud. Sooner or later, you've got to face up to this man."

"You think I don't have the sand to face him, Ike?"

"I didn't say that, Bud, but . . . uh, it kind of looks that way, doesn't it?"

"Would you?" Selvy asked with a trace of asperity.

Coolidge flushed. He glanced around the room defensively. "That isn't the point. I don't have to, after all."

"I didn't mean you lacked the guts, Ike," Selvy said quietly. "The point is, it's not that simple. You take Bitter Creek. We have a peaceful town here. We've worked hard to make it that way, to keep it the kind of place families would want to come to and settle down in, where a woman can feel safe and know her young ones are safe. We've got a fine church and a school. We've kept the violent element out of Bitter Creek. You have any idea what it would do to this town if the story got out about hired guns prowling the streets, shooting and killing? And this Rorke —you don't know him. He shot a man down over there in Colorado just on a whim that had nothin' to do with me. He's a mean, cold-blooded son of a bitch who'd just as soon shoot you as look at you. You don't want him here. Best way to make certain he rides right on through is for me to be gone. I don't know what price the Bascombs have put on my head, but you can bet your last gold piece Rorke won't collect most of it until the job's done, so he won't lose any time here when he finds I've lit out." Selvy paused to let his sober argument sink in. "No, the best thing for this town is for me to sell out, pull up stakes, and move along."

"Suppose you were to put this gunman down," Isiah Howarth said unexpectedly. The newpsaperman was a thoughtful man, and he showed as much now. "The town could ride it out then."

"And the next one? The Bascombs won't stop with one. If Rorke can't do the job, they'll send another. And another after him. Let's face it, Isiah, I won't put 'em all down. But before the parade's over, Bitter Creek will be a spot of dust any sensible family will steer a long course around."

The reasonableness of Selvy's position seemed incontestable. No man found a solid objection. Their eyes met and moved away, half guiltily. They studied Selvy with undiminished respect. He was a man caught in a tight place, and it could have been any one of them. More than one wondered if, in Selvy's boots, he would have given as much thought to his friends and neighbors, and to the survival of their town, as Selvy had.

"I don't see any way around it, gentlemen," Selvy said. "If you take it that I'm showin' yellow in my spine, well, I can't quarrel with what a man thinks when he has what looks to him like good reason. But I think you all know me better than that." Selvy surprised the group by suddenly chuckling. The familiar twinkle reappeared in his blue eyes. "But if you want all the cards up, my friends, I'd have to confess I wouldn't stand much more chance going up alone against this man Rorke than a schoolmarm in a swearin' contest. I can be a hairy bear in an honest fight, but I'm sure enough no Wesley Hardin with a six-gun."

Selvy couldn't have known it, surely, but the germ of the

Reception Committee was planted in that moment. It was nourished a short time later when the meeting broke up. "I'll take the first good offers I get, gentlemen," he said. "But you'd best think it over and get 'em up quick. By this time tomorrow I expect to be far enough down the road for my dust to have settled. Think it over, and do what you think's right; I'll admit you've got me over a barrel for any hard bargaining. And I think it might be a good idea to keep this talk amongst us friends. No need to start up a town scare over this."

They all shook hands with Selvy on the way out, all except Dick Sanderson, who caught Selvy's gesture indicating that he should stay behind. Ike Coolidge, for one, found himself thinking that it took sand, *real* sand, for any man to make the choice Selvy had made, and he shook Selvy's hand with a feeling of genuine sadness and regret. Bitter Creek needed men like Selvy. It was a sorry moment when a hired killer could force him to move on. It was the town's loss . . . and a personal loss for Ike Coolidge.

It occurred to him then that Selvy's account in the bank had grown to be one of his largest. Who would run the general store with equal success? And wasn't the freight line likely to go under without Selvy to ramrod it? And what about Dick Sanderson's grain business? Sanderson's drinking, neglect, and general poor judgment had almost run that concern into the ground before Selvy stepped in as his partner—an arrangement that was supposed to be secret but could hardly hope to escape Coolidge's sharp scrutiny of the town's affairs.

It was a sorry affair, and Coolidge went down the steps from the balcony frowning, carrying a load of worry that became heavier with each step.

Dick Sanderson, lingering after the others had departed, received a real surprise. Selvy placed a big hand on his shoulder and grinned in friendly fashion. "Cheer up, Dick. Listen, I know you don't have enough in the bank to buy me out, the way things are. This thing's come up too sudden. But I don't want to see anyone else move in and take over what you've worked so hard for. So what I've been thinkin' is, why don't we let our little arrangement go on the way it's been. You run the business without me, and you can set aside what's due me as a partner. Then if all this trouble blows over some day, why, maybe I can come back. And if it don't, or if this Rorke or some other hired gun catches me in his sights, then it's all yours and nobody the wiser. You'll be a lucky man that day, Dick."

Sanderson swallowed hard. "I don't call that luck, Mr. Selvy. Hell, no! God damn it, I don't call that luck at all!"

Selvy gave his shoulder a squeeze and shoved him playfully toward the door. "Get along, partner. I got a lot to do in a little space. But that don't mean we won't have time to open another bottle tonight. Stop by here when you close up. I've got a long, thirsty ride ahead of me." Selvy's grin became wistful as a passing thought intruded. "Hell, I'm gonna hate leavin' good friends like you behind. A man don't meet so many along the way that he'd be glad to cross a river with. It won't be easy." Selvy shook his head. "Hell, with friends like I got here in Bitter Creek, standin' shoulder to shoulder with him, a man ought to be able to hold his ground against the whole damn Mexican army. I bet we could at that. But I don't want to see anyone else hurt, Dick, for somethin' that was my doin'. That's the size of it."

They shook hands warmly and Sanderson left, deeply moved.

He carried with him the idea which, though Sanderson did not realize it, Bud Selvy had planted.

Sanderson didn't have that drink with Bud Selvy Wednesday night. Instead he was closeted with Ike Coolidge and a group of Selvy's friends in Harvey Parker's office in the Dust Cutter.

Sanderson had visited Ike Coolidge at the bank shortly after closing. There he had earnestly raised the possibility of Selvy's friends standing shoulder to shoulder with him against the hired killer. The banker, who had been contemplating the losses Selvy's departure from Bitter Creek would mean to him, seized the suggestion eagerly.

Later Ike Coolidge came to think of the idea of the Reception Committee as his own. Oh, Sanderson had said something about helping Selvy out, and the notion was surely in the minds of others who had heard Selvy's startling story that afternoon. But it was Coolidge who acted, Coolidge who came up with a concrete plan.

Before nightfall he had sent word to Isiah Howarth and Alfred Williams to join him and Sanderson at the Dust Cutter for an urgent meeting. Coolidge also invited Jud Falls, a lawyer and former Confederate cavalry officer, hoping to call upon his military experience, but of those who attended, Falls was the only one who later had second thoughts and found excuse to be absent from Bitter Creek for several days. Coolidge enlisted the reluctant support of Harvey Parker, owner of the Dust Cutter. Although Parker refused to join the committee for the expected shoot-out at the stables, he volunteered to have Bud Selvy hide out in his office at the saloon. The office was accessible only through a single door, reached by going past the stairs; it could easily be guarded.

Finally, because Coolidge grasped the advisability of having some lawful sanction for the Reception Committee, he brought Ralph Reese into the group. It was just as well, Coolidge thought, that Ed Crowder was out of town, on the trail of some rustlers who had been working over brands in the back country to the southwest. The sheriff was a hardheaded, no-nonsense lawman who wouldn't have tolerated the suggestion of vigilante action. He would have squelched the Reception Committee before it was born. Deputy Reese was of another breed. Not really of much account, he was useful to Crowder as a Saturday-night deputy, strong and tough enough to shepherd drunken cowhands whose escapades got out of hand, or simply as guardian of the jail in Crowder's absence. Reese was eager to join the committee not only because he was anxious to curry favor with Coolidge, but also because he was the kind of man quick to recognize the aura of success and potential power in Bud Selvy. Reese readily grasped the advantage to himself of having someone like Selvy owe him a favor.

When Ike Coolidge presented his plan for vigilante action, and gave his arguments for it, there was surprisingly little opposition. Bud Selvy was a good friend to each man present, and his sober assessment of his predicament that afternoon had won their sympathy. Besides, if the town let him be run off, they would all suffer . . . and so would the town's reputation. Bitter Creek would be fair game for any other bully boy with a quick draw.

"The way I see it," Coolidge argued, "this should be a town action. This committee will act for the town, and for that reason, Bud Selvy should be kept out of any action we take. He won't be in on the showdown. That way, he can't be charged with anything, and no one's going to try to bring charges against all of us if we act together. The town has a right to defend itself against lawlessness, and that's what we'll be doing."

"Why don't I jist hole up there near the pass with a rifle?" Ralph Reese drawled, enjoying his role among these substantial citizens. "I know me some good places, and I can jist pick off this buscadero 'fore he gits close enough to know I'm there."

"I thought of that," Coolidge admitted. "But I don't think it's a good idea. I believe this has to be a committee action, with no one knowing who fired the bullet that actually puts this gunman down. Besides, if he's the kind of man we think he is, your solution might not work as easily as you think, Reese. This man Rorke might not let himself be picked off, and then he'd be warned. No, we have to set a trap and let him ride into it, in a situation where there's no way he can escape."

"But will that be the end of it?" Isiah Howarth speculated. Howarth welcomed any verbal skirmish or contest of wills, but the thought of participating in an ambush in which a man would be killed came hard to him. "After all, Selvy himself says these Wyoming people will simply hire themselves another gun."

"That might be," Coolidge answered. "But look at it this way. If word gets back to Wyoming, and I expect it will, what will that word be? Not that Selvy has turned the tables on this hireling. The message we'll be sending is that the whole town did it, and that should be plain enough. They might send another killer if it was Selvy alone, but will they send one knowing he has to go against this whole town? I think not. And they might find it a bit harder to find a man willing to take on such an assignment. No, it's my belief that if we do this right, the affair will end there and then. And Bud Selvy will be able to stay on as one of us without having to look over his shoulder for the rest of his days!"

There were few other worries voiced until Jud Falls, who had not been present at Selvy's Mercantile that afternoon, spoke up. "How do we know we have the straight of it from Selvy? After all, we have only his word on any of this. For all we know, it could be the law that's after him."

Coolidge and several others stared at him with distaste. "Well, Jud, I admit we have only Selvy's word," the banker said, "but that's good enough for me. We know he was ready to pull out rather than let this town be hurt. That's important because it says a lot about what kind of man he is. What's more, Dick Sanderson here has seen this hired gunman, and we know the kind he is. He wears no badge. He's a tie-down man for sure, and he doesn't pretend to be anything else. I don't think we have to worry about that part of it, and I'm sure if you'd heard Selvy's story like the rest of us from his own lips, you wouldn't question it."

"I'd still question the legality of what you propose to do," Falls grumbled.

"Legality be damned!" Dick Sanderson said hotly. "Bud Selvy is one of us, and this gunman is an outsider. That ought to be good enough for any of us."

The chorus of agreement firmly quieted Jud Falls. Pleased, Ike Coolidge called on Sanderson to describe the killer so there would be no doubt about the man they were setting their trap for. Sanderson, feeling his importance and excited by his unique role in the developing drama, recounted Burt Angstrom's impressions of the hired killer as well as his own observations. He described Rorke as being tall and thin, mean-faced, and wearing two guns tied low, dressed mostly in black and easy to spot. Moreover, while Sanderson had been waiting for the stage in Colton, he had seen the gunman's horse, a big chestnut with a white apron.

"That's the man we're after," Ike Coolidge said when Sanderson sat down. "Sanderson will be one of us, so there should be no mistake. The man sounds easy enough to identify. And I think, if we're all agreed, we can promise him a warm reception! In fact," Coolidge added as growing enthusiasm brought general exclamations of approval, "I suggest that's what we call ourselves officially—the Reception Committee!"

The Reception Committee, Tug Walsh thought, still lying belly down in the bed of his wagon in the darkness of the livery-stable yard. It was a good enough name, and the gunman had had his welcome. Trouble was, the committee was really a bunch of cubs snapping at the heels of a genuine he-bear. And Walsh had a feeling, deep in his gut,

that before this night was over more than one of the cubs
was going to be badly clawed.

Walsh scowled, baffled by the fixes a man could get himself into without much deliberation. The truth was that he
didn't much like Bud Selvy. What everyone else seemed to
admire, Selvy's unfailing cheerfulness, sometimes rubbed
Walsh the wrong way. His was a hard, grinding life. There
was laughter in it, and it surely had its blessings, but
neither was as common as thorns in the desert—or Selvy's
grin. Most of the time, from sunup to sunset, Tug Walsh
didn't find much to grin about. After a while you began
to wonder about a man who laughed too much, just as you
wondered about one who never laughed at all.

The cattleman wasn't risking a bullet in the dark because he liked Selvy; he was there because Selvy was to be
his neighbor. Because a man stood with his neighbor
against an unjust or unequal threat, whether he liked him
or not. And—perhaps more important than any of the
other reasons—because Walsh hated the kind of man who
was little more than a fist at the butt end of a gun, a man
who hired himself out to kill, without anger, without pity,
and without regret.

Pensively Walsh studied the two lanterns near the stable
doors. The hanging lantern was too close to be shot out.
Too much risk of a fire. The other, sitting on the stump
where Whitey Smith had placed it, might safely be smashed.

What was certain to Walsh was that there was no way to
move past those lights through the doorway. One way or
another, they had to be snuffed out.

Slowly Walsh eased backward, released the tail gate of
the spring wagon, and slipped quietly to the ground. He
studied the barn and the shadows of the yard. Howarth
was close by, and the darkness along this south side of the
yard was reassuring. It should be possible for either Howarth or Walsh himself to reach Ike Coolidge at the corner
of the barn without risk.

Keeping low, Walsh crept past some corral poles toward the horse trough where Isiah Howarth crouched. To his left, a horse nickered and moved, acknowledging his presence. The horses had been released earlier from the stables for their own safety. Walsh was reminded now of the stranger's chestnut. Had he been struck in that first volley of wild shooting? Hard to tell. The horse had bolted briefly, skittering across the yard, swinging clear of the board fence on the north side and angling toward the fork in the road that led either into town or back along the wagon road west. But he was a steady animal, it seemed, and he had not run far. Calming quickly, he had pulled up and waited. After a while he had drifted back toward the edge of the yard, where Walsh could see him now. He was about ten yards behind the woodpile where Ralph Reese waited. Seeing no way for the killer to reach his horse and make a run, Walsh returned his attention to the barn and the problem of the man trapped inside.

"Howarth?" he called ahead in low warning. "It's me—Walsh. I'm comin' up."

He saw Howarth jerk around in alarm, his carbine banging against an edge of the trough as it swung with his movement. Walsh was grateful for the caution that had made him call out. The little newspaperman was still jittery.

Walsh went down on his haunches beside Howarth, who turned a narrow, sharp-featured face toward him. "You think Williams hit him like he says?"

"Could be."

"You don't sound convinced."

"He might be scratched, but I wouldn't count on him bein' laid up."

Howarth nodded. "He moved fast. He must have smelled it coming, I think. I didn't think I could miss him at this range, but by the time I squeezed off he wasn't where I aimed."

The rancher grunted. "If he's the kind of hardcase he's supposed to be, it didn't figger to be easy."

"We've got him trapped in there, though."

"Yeah," Walsh said without enthusiasm. "Now all we have to do is smoke him out." He didn't sound as if he thought that would be any easier.

"Fire the barn?" Howarth was aghast. "Sanderson and Whitey are in there—and Williams!"

"Hell, no," Walsh growled. Anyone firing up a building on the edge of town in the middle of this long dry spell would have to have a whisky-soaked or addled brain. There was enough wind to carry sparks to nearby roofs, and it wouldn't take much more to level the entire business district once a real fire got started. "But we can't risk lettin' him slip away. I don't like it, but we're gonna have to flush him out."

Howarth reflected unhappily on this judgment. "That means . . . someone has to go in after him, doesn't it?"

Walsh did not reply. It struck him that Howarth was nervous, even scared, but still ready to do what had to be done. The little newspaperman was a scrapper.

"It's more than I bargained for," Howarth said.

"Somethin' like this generally is," Walsh said, a little impatiently. Too much soul searching at such a time was dangerous. "I'm gonna try to reach that hanging lantern first. If I can blow it, you think you can cover me whilst I go for the one on the stump?"

"I can," Howarth said firmly, without hesitation.

"I'll let Coolidge know what I'm up to. You stay here and cover the yard. Once the lights are out, he may try to make a run for his horse. That's him standin' over there. We can't let that happen."

Isiah Howarth nodded. He didn't have to be told what it might mean if the gunman escaped on horseback. He would be free to lick his wounds until he was ready to come back, at his own time and in his own way, to repay those who had bushwhacked him.

Tug Walsh made out the oval of Coolidge's pale face turned toward them. The banker had heard them. Relieved that he didn't have to worry about another nervous trigger finger, Walsh ran forward and dropped to the ground beside Coolidge at the corner of the barn. Briefly he outlined his plan.

"Why put out the lights?" Coolidge protested. "If he comes out that way now, we can see him, but—"

"He won't," Walsh cut in curtly. "Not the way it is. He's no fool. That should be plain enough."

He watched the banker chew this over. Coolidge seemed to him a gray kind of man, without emotion or color of any kind. He was helpless on a horse and made no pretense of trying to ride one. Walsh had never seen him drunk or excited or with a woman, or heard any vices attributed to him, unless it was greed. In money matters, Ike Coolidge was known to be both shrewd and tough. Only inside his bank did he seem to be fully himself, out of the sun, absorbed in his bloodless passion. Certainly he was out of place at the holding end of a shotgun, the leader of a vigilante bunch.

"That makes sense," Coolidge admitted. "But I don't see how it can help us if we can't see him."

"It means he can't see us neither. I'm goin' in that barn. There's no other way. I'll have Reese to back me up, and Sanderson and Williams on the inside. You and Howarth will have to cover the escape holes."

Coolidge's face seemed to turn paler in the dim light. "That's dangerous, surely. There must be some other way . . ."

"If there is, I can't think what it is. It's got to be done, and we can't give him time to think. We give him too much of that already."

"What about asking him to throw out his gun and come out? He must know he doesn't stand much chance, one man against so many."

Tug Walsh stared at the banker speculatively, wondering at the naïvete of the question. "What kind of promise you figger to make him?" There was an undercurrent in the cowman's query, and Ike Coolidge did not fail to hear it. Walsh would not stand for a broken promise, one made only to lure the gunfighter into the open where he could be cold-bloodedly gunned down. The initial ambush had compromised Walsh's simple code of honor more than he had wanted to admit, and he would go no further.

"I . . . I don't know." There was a moment's silence. Then Coolidge asked, "What . . . what do you want me to do?" The question was an acknowledgment that the banker knew he was out of his element and that Tug Walsh had taken over direction of the Reception Committee.

"I figger he'll try to make a run," Walsh said. "We'll have too many guns comin' at him, no matter how much of a lead thrower he is. There's only three ways out of that barn that I know of. Through the front, and we'll be comin in that way. Anyways, Howarth will cover it. Then there's the side door back here, lets into the corral. That's yours to watch. If anybody comes out that way, don't wait to ask him his name or the time of day. Just cut loose. Only other door is out back. It lets into Whitey's saddle room and he keeps a padlock on it. He's had too many things turn up missin' before he put that lock there. When I go in, I'll head that way so's I can block him off. But I don't figger he'd know about that door, and if he did find it and come up against a lock, I doubt he'd fool around with it in the dark. Looks to me like he'll either have to hole up and shoot it out, or he'll come out one of these two ways, yours or up front." The cowman paused. "When he does, he won't give nobody time to think."

"I understand. You can count on me. . . . I won't miss this time."

The banker seemed relieved by his assignment. And with good reason, Tug Walsh thought sourly, wondering again how he had let himself be talked into joining this wild bunch.

It did not occur to him, even then, to pick up and walk away from the affair, preserving his own skin whole.

He looked across the yard. One of the two lanterns he had to take out was suspended from an iron hook, fortunately on the near side of the wide entrance. Reaching it seemed safe enough except for one fact: The outside light would be visible through normal gaps in the wall of the barn. If the gunman inside was in the right position, he might be able to see a shadow filling those cracks as Walsh moved along the wall.

Tug Walsh sucked in a deep breath and let it out slowly, releasing some of the jittery tension in his body. He was committed now, and he couldn't allow himself to start thinking too much or worrying about the consequences of a hasty decision already made. It did no more good to worry about what might be than to fret over what had been.

With a brief final nod, the cattleman turned away from Ike Coolidge. He had to trust in the banker keeping his nerve along with Howarth and Williams and Reese, even though it gave him the feeling of stepping out over a deep chasm on a thin board with visible cracks. There was simply no other way across this chasm. As for Sanderson, the only thing Walsh could hope for there was that Dick wouldn't ventilate him instead of the killer they were after.

Walsh kept low to shrink his shadow. He could feel his heart hammering; blood pounded in his eardrums. He was a little surprised that the gunman hadn't thrown more lead before this. He was a cool one, biding his time. Walsh had known such men, and he knew they were the worst kind to face in any fire fight. When such a man acted, he struck swiftly and with deadly purpose.

Walsh stopped behind a rain barrel. The lantern on its wall support was ten feet away. Walsh's mouth felt dry, and in spite of himself he licked his lips, feeling the dry grate of his tongue.

The gunman in the barn might be waiting for him to

reach for the lantern, he thought. He would be a tall target then, full in the light.

Walsh glanced across the yard, wondering if Ralph Reese had figured out what he was up to. Probably so, assuming that the deputy had remained sober enough to pay attention. Reese wasn't very predictable or reliable, but the strong desire to curry favor which had made him so eager to join the vigilantes should have kept him from emptying his bottle too quickly. Maybe.

Walsh wished that Ed Crowder had been in town this day. No doubt he would have flayed some skin off various members of the Reception Committee with his tongue and put an end to all this before it started.

But Crowder would have faced the gunfighter alone. The sheriff wouldn't have let anyone ride into Bitter Creek to gun down one of the town's citizens without a challenge. Crowder was good, but he wasn't young any more. Maybe the committee's way was best, after all.

Except that they hadn't done the job.

Walsh sucked his belly against his spine and went for the hanging lantern. He felt the cold neck-grip of fear as he reached high. He grabbed the lantern, pulled . . . and the wire-loop handle caught on the iron cradle.

Walsh's whole body flinched. For an instant he stood frozen. Then, swearing softly, he lifted the loop clear, brought the lantern down, and blew it.

As he sank once again into a crouch, questions pounded at him. Why hadn't the gunman acted? Was he hidden somewhere deep in the barn? Was he unwilling to show where he was? Was he nursing his wound in a stall out of sight of the doorway, or behind some barricade that wouldn't let him risk peering out?

Tug Walsh gave a fatalistic shrug, accepting what he had to do, acknowledging that he couldn't answer any of these questions or peer into the unknown killer's mind. He looked at the remaining lantern on its sawed-off stump. It was two jumps away.

Wiping his mind clean of all the possibles, Walsh leaped toward the remaining light, swooped down, and blew it out.

He hit the dirt and kept rolling. When he bounced to his feet, he was on the run. He raced past the wide double doors on a weaving course that carried him across the yard to the woodpile where Ralph Reese watched him, open-mouthed.

Dropping beside the deputy, breathing hard, Tug Walsh spoke angrily, angry with himself for his fear, suddenly angrier than before at the stranger in the barn. "I'm goin' in there. You got to back me up, Reese."

"Go inside? Godalmighty, Walsh—"

"You heard me, damn it! You want to let him break out so's he can come after you his own way?"

In the darkness Reese stared at him. He hadn't looked that far ahead. Now that Walsh forced him to, he didn't like what he saw.

"I'll go in first," Walsh said grimly. "You come in behind." When he heard the deputy swallow hard, the cowman reached out and grabbed a fistful of shirt. Reese was a big, strong man, bigger than Walsh, but Walsh knew that if the deputy had shown any yellow in that moment, he would have whipped him. "You sounded mighty eager an hour back, and you must have some excuse for wearin' that tin badge. I'm goin' in, and if you ain't behind me when I get there, you better find your own horse and start ridin', and don't never stop inside of Texas."

Reese swiped his hand away. "Hell, Walsh, I'll back you," he said, his tone aggrieved.

Tug Walsh stared at him for another moment. Then he turned toward the barn. Beyond the open doors was a black pit, and he liked it no better than Reese did. But Walsh was a doggedly determined man. Once he had committed himself to a fight, nothing would make him back off. The man inside the barn could have been the devil himself, howling like thunder and spitting out bolts of lightning, and Tug Walsh would have gone to meet him.

He was conscious of the black darkness all around the livery stables and of a taut silence pierced by the whistle of a quail from a nearby field. He gathered himself as he had before, biting off his fear and sucking in his breath. Then he charged across the yard.

He reached the barn entrance on the dead run and hurled himself into the blackness. He knew the inside of the stables almost as well as he knew his own bunkhouse, and he knew that the nearest stall opposite the entrance had been empty when the committee took up its vigil. He dived for the stall without seeing it. He landed on his shoulder on a thin bed of straw and moist droppings. The soggy layer skidded under him. He skated hard against the back of the stall.

Behind him Reese pounded through the open doorway and scuttled for cover.

For several seconds Tug Walsh lay motionless, heart pounding, chest heaving. Somehow his six-gun had jumped into his hand, and his thumb was on the hammer.

But nothing happened.

Slowly Walsh's earlier questions returned. Where was the wounded gunman? Why hadn't he fired at the first man through the doorway? Had he been hurt worse than Walsh had thought? Or was he coolly waiting until he had located all of his adversaries before he chose to fight?

"Walsh?" Reese called out anxiously. "You okay?"

The cattleman didn't answer. If the killer had not already placed him in his stall, Walsh was not going to make it easy for him. But even as this thought formed, another chased it from his mind. *The killer would take no heed because the killer wasn't there.*

Then he heard movement at the far end of the stables, the south end, and in the same instant saw the red spurt of flame from the muzzle of Ralph Reese's rifle as he fired.

Over the echoing crash of the shot, someone screamed.

FOUR

As he threw himself from the saddle, Owen Conagher felt something tug at his left side. Gunfire exploded all around him. He saw powder flashes off to his left and above him as well as from within the barn.

Instinct drove him forward without thought. He seemed to be sprinting right into the muzzle of a gun inside the stables. For some reason, his left leg caved under him, and he felt himself falling out of control. He had lost his hat, and the last shot from the gun in one of the stalls close by put a new part in his shock of thick black hair.

Conagher sprawled flat and rolled, breathless and bewildered. Somewhere to his left, someone was scrambling frantically away from him, and he thought with fleeting anger of the little balding truth seeker with the lantern. He had known what was coming. With his light he had lured Conagher into an ambush.

There was no time for anger or even for wondering why. More shots followed him into the barn, and there was confused shouting over the explosive uproar. Conagher made out a blacksmith's anvil nearby, a fire pit and some benches, but he didn't linger. This area was too open. He sought deeper shadows and better cover.

He knew he had been hit. There was a stickiness at his side, at the bottom of the rib cage, and his leg, at first numb, telegraphed hot flashes of pain as he drove himself across the dirt floor into a horse stall. In some recess of his mind he noted that the stall was empty, that all of the stalls were empty of animals, and added this to the catalogue of evidence that the ambush had been carefully set up for him ahead of time.

A single shot crashed. Conagher heard the bullet smack into wood a few feet away.

That came from overhead. Someone staked out in the loft. The knowledge brought a new chill, for the loft overlooked too much of the stables.

He found a loose board at the back of the stall when it yielded to the pressure of his shoulder. He felt a broken end and a gap, and quickly traced the size of the opening with his hand. It was wide enough for a thin man to squeeze through.

Conagher felt that he had to keep moving, that he couldn't let his ambushers know for certain where he was. For the moment, the darkness inside the stables had saved him, but there were too many guns drawn against him for that safety to last.

Working slowly, to avoid as much noise as possible, he began to worm through the opening at the back of the stall. Movement brought a stab to his side, like the stitch of a man out of breath. And when his left leg scraped across the jagged end of the broken board, he had to bite his lip against a gasp of pain.

A layer of straw in the next stall cushioned his fall as he tumbled through the gap. Now a barricade loomed between him and the lighted entrance, and the stall in which he lay was dark as a well.

Conagher lay still, drawing shallow breaths. For the first time since the instinct of danger had hurled him from his horse, he thought of pulling his own six-gun and throwing lead back at his attackers. Yet he made no move toward his Colt. He didn't know who was shooting at him, but they had given him cause enough to fire back. What stayed him was a motive stronger than anger. Common sense told him that he would not survive a shoot-out against so many when he didn't know where they were—or how many.

In the first burst of fire, he had counted four or five different gun flashes, at least two from inside the stables. There might have been more.

Conagher would fight when he had to. And if he had to go out this way, not knowing why, he would make more than one of his bushwhackers regret their welcome. They might have him backed into a corner soon enough. In the meantime, however, he wanted to know more.

For a full five minutes Conagher lay motionless in the dark, ignoring the sweat that ran into his eyes, indifferent to the assortment of scraped skin patches and banged bones he had picked up during his plunge into the stables, and examining with a cool curiosity the pain that centered in his side and particularly in his left leg. During the interval, he learned a surprising amount of information about his attackers.

There was one more flurry of shots, capped by exultant shouts from the loft almost directly overhead. That waddy had a high-pitched voice with a funny accent, but the language was English and the reason for the triumphant cry was clear. The man upstairs thought he had hit Conagher with one of his shots. Conagher was fairly sure he hadn't. The bullet that had creased his side as well as the one that seemed to have lodged itself in his leg had been fired from closer to ground level if he was any judge. The latter had come at the moment Conagher was diving through the doorway, and it certainly had not come from above. Not that it mattered. What counted was that the shouting enabled him to place the Englishman in the loft fairly accurately—close enough to put a bullet through the floor boards where the man was stationed.

Conagher had also pinpointed the locations of two of the men outside, though he was certain that more than two were there. He knew that the balding stableman called Whitey was cowering at the south end of the barn. He knew also that there was one other armed man inside the stables with him. His name was Sanderson—the man in the loft had called out to him.

Conagher decided to move when he heard that stalwart bushwhacker shift his weight and scrape a toe against a board. Sanderson was in one of the front stalls to the right of the entrance as you came in. His was the gun muzzle Conagher had waded into. For good reason, this fact made their relationship more personal.

Owen Conagher had lived with Indians, and he could move with the stealthy cunning of an Apache. He had also fought Apaches, as a tracker with the cavalry in the war and after. A dozen years of fending for himself, surviving a multitude of scrapes, hadn't dulled his senses or cost him his ability to stalk game or a man with no more heavy-footedness than a hungry cat.

Slowly he removed his boots. He carried them with him for a short distance after leaving his stall. Then he found a door leading into a back room and he placed the boots by the post at the right side of the door, where he could find them in a hurry.

In his stockinged feet—one toe poked through a hole— he crept closer to the nervous man in the front stall. Conagher knew Sanderson was nervous because he kept having to clear his throat, and each time he did, he was a little noisier about it. Sanderson was worried and impatient and, Conagher guessed, he was wondering about the victim of the ambush, trying to decide if he was well and truly shot up and no longer a hazard. But Sanderson wasn't sure, and so far he wasn't ready to gamble on the chance.

Conagher slithered the last few feet along the floor until he reached the stall that backed up to the one where Sanderson crouched. He made no sound. When he was inside the stall, no more than six feet from his attacker, Conagher paused for a full minute, motionless. He waited until Sanderson moved again, rubbing some leather that creaked faintly, then clearing his dry throat.

Conagher eased closer. He had no worry now about being seen. The darkness close to the floor among the stalls was almost total. Sound was his only concern.

At last he was against the back wall, his shoulder touching it. He could feel the blood soaking his shirt and seeping slowly through his jeans. His slow progress along the floor had encouraged fresh bleeding. The wound in his leg was the worse, and it was having all kinds of dirt ground into it, but it seemed to Conagher that the pain wasn't bad enough to suggest that any bones had been smashed. He had probed the wound in his side with his fingers and was sure that there was only a shallow trough where a bullet had passed by. He had been lucky enough, so far.

"Sanderson? You all right?" The Englishman in the loft called down anxiously.

"Yeah."

"I think I hit him."

Sanderson didn't reply. It was easier to be confident, Conagher thought, when you were safe in the loft . . . or thought yourself safe.

"What about the others?" the Englishman asked. "Perhaps if we all rushed this fellow—"

"Shut up," Sanderson snapped.

In the darkness only a few feet away, Owen Conagher grinned wolfishly. Sanderson was uneasy, perhaps without knowing why. A man who has been close to danger often enough respected such instincts better. For his own part, Conagher was able, through the smells of urine and old droppings and straw and leathers that permeated the stables, to smell the worried man on the other side of the barrier. Probably Sanderson smelled *him* without knowing it.

Cautiously Conagher began to unfold his long body, drawing himself erect. He brought an eye over the top of the low wall separating the stalls. A quick glance toward the loft at the front of the barn told him the Englishman wasn't visible.

Conagher stood to his full height. Gently he drew his Colt from the leather holster. It slid from the slick, hard leather, polished by years of use, without a sound.

The wall was about five feet high and Conagher was able to look over it easily. Sanderson was directly below, hunched against the side of his stall well toward the back, away from the aisle.

"Ssst!" Conagher hissed.

Sanderson looked up, startled, as Conagher clubbed downward with the long barrel of his Colt. He saw Sanderson open his mouth to cry out, but he was too late. The thunk of the barrel striking bone was muffled by Sanderson's hat, but the blow was solid.

Without a sound, Sanderson slid sideways to the floor.

Conagher sank back into the shadows of the rear stall. He listened for any sounds of Sanderson stirring. There were none. He had struck hard, Conagher thought without remorse, because he had known the force of the blow would be cushioned by that fine-looking Stetson. Sanderson should sleep for some time.

By this time Conagher had concluded that Sanderson was the only one of his attackers inside the stable, other than the man in the loft and Whitey Smith. The latter didn't figure as one of the combatants in this fight. His job had ended when the shooting started.

That situation didn't seem likely to last for long. If someone didn't decide to fire the barn to smoke him out, they would charge him sooner or later. It might take some time for a bunch of sidewinding backshot artists to work up enough sand for a straight-up battle, but their very nervousness would eventually drive them to it. They would be afraid to leave him alive in the barn.

Thoughtfully Conagher considered the satisfactions of putting a bullet through the boards of the loft at the point where he had placed the man with the English accent. He decided against it. There was no delight in him for random killing, even of men who had earned it. And his shot would tell the hellers outside more than he wanted them to know. As of now they couldn't be certain where he was or what condition he was in. It was better to keep them uncertain.

He decided it was time to investigate that back room.

His boots were where he had left them beside the narrow plank door. He drew them on, wincing at the pain renewed when he put strain on his leg and the stab under his ribs when he bent over. With searching fingers he traced the hole in the meaty underside of his thigh. His jeans were sodden. He worked his bandanna over the wound, pulled it tight around his leg, and knotted it.

The barn was quiet. There was a string latch on the plank door, and it released noiselessly. Conagher opened the door an inch at a time, holding his breath, waiting for a betraying creak of hinges. But Whitey kept his hinges well oiled, and the door swung inward in silence. Conagher stepped through and softly closed the door behind him.

The room was black. Smells of saddle and gear told him he was in a harness room. There was a deeply scarred bench where leather was evidently cut and worked and repaired. He felt his way along the bench. Cracks in the far wall told him which way to go and how far, for the night sky was brighter than the interior of the stables.

He found the exit he had hoped for.

And a heavy padlock securing it.

Conagher's careful movements had acquainted him with the outlines of the room even in the darkness, and it took him only a short time to find and examine by touch the various tools on the bench or set into wall hooks and holders made for them. The stableman was a neat, orderly sort of fellow, Conagher thought approvingly. He located a hammer, a big screwdriver, a tin of nails, an awl, a couple of knives, and some sort of metal punch. None of these seemed adequate for breaking out.

Then, hanging in a corner above one end of the bench, he found a long pair of heavy iron tongs.

Conagher hefted the tongs with satisfaction. He didn't hope to break open that solid padlock, but the door itself seemed less sturdy. The wood was old, and—

Something caught his attention, stirring the small hairs at the back of his neck. It took a second or two before he realized what it was. There had been faint light behind him, always visible through various cracks in the stable walls, coming from those two lanterns set out front. That light had dimmed.

Then it vanished completely. The second of the two lanterns had been blown.

In that instant Conagher knew the attack was coming.

Moving more quickly now, heedless of any minor noise he might make, he rammed the handle of the tongs into the iron loop that held the padlock. He tested it, leaning all of his weight back, using the long handles of the tongs as a lever. The muscles of his arms and shoulders and back bulged with strain. Pain tore at his side.

Something cracked. Wood yielded, splintering. The lock was breaking away.

Conagher paused then, waiting, certain that it would not be long. He heard the rush of one man, then another into the stables. One of them slammed hard against a wall, the impact clearly audible. Conagher's teeth showed white in the darkness of the harness room as he grinned.

Then a rifle boomed and he heaved back with all of his strength. Lock and brace broke away from the door and it seemed to bounce open. Conagher went through the opening fast, into the cool and welcome night.

"Oh, my God, boys, don't shoot! It's me—Whitey!"

Tug Walsh swore vividly as he made out the figure crawling across the stable floor toward him. From outside came a single shot, and he quickened toward it. Then he brushed it aside; no one had gone past him through the front doors. That had been Howarth's shot, and he had nothing to shoot at.

"It's me, boys!" Whitey Smith implored them again. "Don't send me over!"

Walsh stepped out of his stall, still cautious but convinced that there was no longer any danger inside the barn. He heard Reese move up beside him.

"Where the hell did he get to?" the deputy wondered aloud. "God damn it, Whitey, you *oughta* be dead, crawlin' out like that."

It was Walsh who wondered about Sanderson, not heard from since the killer had disappeared into the stables. He began a hasty search and soon found Sanderson slumped on the floor of one of the front stalls. By then, Alfred Williams was leaning over the edge of the loft, calling down eagerly, and Ike Coolidge had appeared in the front entrance, followed by Isiah Howarth.

"Who's that?" Coolidge asked worriedly.

"Sanderson."

"Is he . . . uh . . . dead?"

"He's still breathin'." There was an egg-sized lump on Sanderson's skull, and Walsh thought his chest fluttered unevenly when he put a hand over the man's heart, but he was alive.

And lucky, Walsh thought, wondering anew about the killer they had tried to gun down, a gunman who had not fired a single shot.

The cattleman organized a careful, thorough search of the stables, two men working together to cover each section. Only when the team of Reese and Williams found the padlock broken away from the back door of the harness room did he relax enough to bring one of the lanterns into the stables and strike a match to it.

The other members of the Reception Committee stared back at him somberly, blinking against the light. Tug Walsh saw anxiety and fear in every face except Reese's. He wondered if the deputy was too stupid to be afraid, or simply bucked up by bottled courage more than the others.

"What does it mean, Walsh?" Isiah Howarth finally asked.

"It means he's flown the coop," the cowman answered impatiently.

"Yes, I know, but . . . won't he come back?"

Walsh looked at the newspaperman grimly, then at Coolidge and Williams and Reese in turn. None of them spoke, as if they were waiting for his reassurance. But they all knew the answer without his telling them.

"He's a gunman," Tug Walsh said bluntly. "He's hurt, because he's left blood around enough to fill a bucket. But he's still strong enough, and he's smart enough, to get away right under our noses. And he won't run, you might as well know that. Not a man like him. We let him get loose, and now we're gonna have to go after him."

"Go after him?" Ike Coolidge repeated, aghast.

"Either that," Walsh said grimly, "or wait for him to come after you. Because he surely will. You and me and every last one of us. We're marked men, every member of this Reception Committee. I didn't take much to this whole notion, but there's no backing away from it now. We got to find him before he finds us, or this town will be diggin' holes to put us in, because he surely means to make us pay. A man like that, a hired gun, couldn't do nothin' else." Walsh paused to read the faces turned toward him in the light of the lantern like a row of sunflowers seeking the sun, each more openly fearful as his harsh words drummed at them. "If we don't bury him quick, he'll bury every one of us!"

FIVE

Dan Colgrove leaned forward in his chair, letting the curve of the rocker bring him close to the porch railing. He cocked his left ear—the good one—toward the west end of town, and waited. There had been a single rifle shot. A moment later came another report, this one lighter, thinner, distinctly the sound of a handgun.

So it wasn't over.

Behind him he heard Willa's step. She appeared in the doorway, her shadow mirrored in the light panel thrown across the porch like an image in a still, sunlit pool.

She moved out onto the porch and paused attentively, like him, listening for more sounds of the fighting.

"I'd hoped it was over," she said.

Her father grunted. His feathers were still ruffled over his putdown by Bud Selvy and the way Willa had sided with Selvy against him.

Maybe that was the whole problem. He hated seeing them as partners, yet he could offer no legitimate defense of his prejudice.

"I hope no one's been hurt."

"Well, you can rest easy over Bud."

"Oh, Pa, you're hopeless! You won't even give him a chance. Maybe you really do want him out of the way because of me. Is that it?"

"Don't talk foolish, and don't get smart with your father."

"What is it, then?"

"You know blamed well what it is. It's this Reception Committee of his, that's what."

"It's not *his* committee. He didn't even want it. You forget I was there in the office when Mr. Coolidge and some of the others came to talk to him. They closed the door, but I heard some of it. Bud didn't cotton to the idea at all."

"For a man who was so much against it, he didn't put up much of a battle, seems like."

She stepped over to the railing in front of him, forcing him to look up at her directly. "Why are you so set against what the committee's doing, anyway? Mr. Selvy didn't ask for this fight—none of them did. It's these Wyoming people, and this gunfighter they sent—they're responsible. They forced it. You hate that kind of man as much as I do, Pa. You can't deny that."

Dan Colgrove was silent a moment. Then he said, thoughtfully, "We've only Dick Sanderson's word about him." And Selvy's, he thought.

"Isn't that good enough? Mr. Sanderson would have no reason to lie about such a thing."

"He wouldn't have to be lying. He could be wrong, that's all. I would never have said that Sanderson was a fine judge of humankind, good or bad. I wouldn't put too much trust in anything he said, even with his hand on the Good Book."

Willa stared at him. "What are you trying to say now?"

Her father waved his hand, as if brushing the question away. He didn't want to quarrel with her, and it seemed that any discussion involving Bud Selvy always turned out that way. Maybe it was his fault after all, always searching for that hidden something in Selvy that struck him wrong, like an almost invisible hitch in a horse's gait that shouldn't have been there unless there was some structural weakness that eluded the eye.

"Well?"

"Nothing."

"No, you can't wriggle out of it that easy. You meant

something. You don't say things like that unless you have something on your mind. What is it?"

He fumbled his pipe out of his pocket along with a leather pouch of tobacco. While he poured the blackened bowl half full, tamped the measure down and topped it off, he felt uneasy. He knew that he was stalling and that Willa was aware of the evasiveness. Striking a match, he squinted against the flaring light. His hand trembled as he touched the flame to the tobacco.

"You'd say anything to turn me against Bud Selvy, wouldn't you?" Willa said quietly.

"That's not—" He puffed agitatedly. "That's not so."

"It won't do any good. You might as well get used to that." She drew herself up to her full height, a tall and lovely young woman with defiance in every line of her body. "Because I'm going to marry him, Pa!"

The match burned his fingers and he dropped it. It sputtered out as it reached the deck. He couldn't look at her. "To spite me?"

"No!" she cried. "Oh, you're just . . ." She couldn't find words.

"I know, I'm hopeless. But if it's not to show me, what is it, then?"

"You know why!"

"Because you love him? It shouldn't be so hard to say if it's true. You just tell me. Tell me right out you love him and that'll be the end of it. You'll never hear me speak another word against him."

Dan Colgrove heard the challenge of his words with a kind of surprise, for he had not intended them. He knew that he was taking a terrible risk even as he spoke, and that his pledge would be hard, if not impossible, to keep. And yet he would not take them back. They had come from his intuitive estimate not only of Selvy but also of his daughter. That unreasoned judgment told him that

Willa was not as certain of her heart as she pretended—nor as sure of Selvy's worth.

Abruptly she turned from him and ran into the house. The door banged behind her, and Dan Colgrove was left in darkness and silence. He listened for her movements within the house, but after a while there was nothing to hear.

Brooding now, Dan turned his attention toward the town. Shifting in his chair, he felt the old, familiar pain in his broken hip, which had never properly healed and had left him crippled, able to hobble around only with the aid of a cane, slowly and painfully. He thought of rising and struggling down from the porch for the walk he forced himself to take each evening, but he did not stir. He wondered what the shots from the direction of the stables had signaled, and, like Willa, he hoped that none of the men of the town who had so bravely styled themselves a Reception Committee to meet a killer had been harmed.

"If he was a man, he'd have been there himself," Dan Colgrove muttered aloud, thinking of Selvy.

Deliberating over these things, worried more than he cared to admit by Willa's reaction, Dan Colgrove failed to see the face that peered around a corner of the porch and, finding him there, briefly withdrew. But his good ear was still acute, and it detected the faint scraping of a boot when the man seized the railing and climbed over it onto the porch.

Colgrove had one hand in his shirt pocket, reaching for a match, and he held it there, motionless. He turned his head slowly and blinked at a tall, rawboned stranger.

"Reachin' for anythin' in particular?" Owen Conagher asked.

"A match."

"Go right ahead then. I never objected to a man smokin' when he felt like it."

Colgrove drew the match and struck it into flame with

his thumbnail. In the flare of the light his eyes were drawn instantly to the stranger's blood-streaked shirt and the sodden bandanna wrapped around his left leg. He held the match to his pipe, and his hand was steady.

"You a pipe smoker?" Colgrove wondered aloud, after his load of tobacco was burning steadily.

"Nope. Never seemed to have the time."

The unexpected answer brought a chuckle from Dan Colgrove. "It does take time." His amusement faded. "Seems like that's all I have any more."

"You don't look old enough to leave behind on a blanket."

Colgrove nodded, understanding the reference to Indian ways when an old one was ready to die. His curiosity about this quiet man who had appeared so unexpectedly with a couple of obvious bullet holes in him was rising. *Sanderson's a fool,* he thought.

"How old would a crippled horse have to be for you to shoot him?" he asked.

The stranger showed his teeth in a smile. There was strain behind the smile, Dan Colgrove thought, but it was genuine all the same. The strain was something else, undoubtedly to do with the lead he had caught.

"I take it you don't get around much," Conagher said.

"Not much."

"That why you wasn't in on the fun down there at the stables a little while back?"

"Maybe." Dan Colgrove puffed thoughtfully on his pipe. This man didn't strike him as a mean one, but there was something coiled and dangerous in him, and Dan had begun to worry about Willa. If this man was the hired killer, which seemed certain, and if she should happen to step back out onto the porch, drawn by their voices . . .

"Is that the way this town always welcomes strangers?"

"Not always," Colgrove retorted testily. "We don't like hired guns, is all."

The tall man released a long, slow breath, and some of the danger seemed to drain out of him at the same time. He nodded slowly. "I figured it had to be somethin' like that."

"You sound like maybe you was expecting trouble."

"No," Conagher said. "But I'm used to it. Is there any real law in this town?"

"Sheriff Crowder's not here. But the deputy was down there at the stables to meet you with the others."

A quick frown darkened the stranger's drawn face. He scrubbed one hand through black hair, as if baffled. "I reckon they was expectin' somebody——"

"You come over from Colton?"

Conagher nodded.

"That's it, then."

"They shoot everybody from Colton?"

"Hell, no!" Dan Colgrove snapped. "You know damned well why they were waiting for you, and why you came here."

The tall man gave an explosive sigh of disgust. "Maybe you'd like to spell it out for me."

"You was hired to gun down Bud Selvy!"

Dan Colgrove watched the stranger closely in the dim light of the porch, but he saw no reaction to Selvy's name, only a wry twist of the tall man's mouth.

"Don't you see it yet, old man?" the stranger murmured. "They bushwhacked the wrong man."

For a long minute Dan Colgrove stared at him. His pipe had gone out, but he made no move to light another match. "They wouldn't make a mistake like that," he said finally, speaking with more conviction than he was beginning to feel. "One of them saw you over in Colton. Heard you asking about Selvy. You call him Asher, I guess. Your story's known, and this town won't stand for any hired guns——"

"I don't know any Selvy. Asher neither," Conagher interrupted wearily. He leaned against the porch railing. "The damned fools. How many people do they figger to shoot before they hit the right one?"

"That's kinda hard to believe . . ."

Dan Colgrove stopped talking because he realized suddenly that he *did* believe this stranger, without evidence to justify his conviction beyond his own knowledge of people, the intuitive judgment that told him this was another kind of man. If there was danger in him, it was born of anger, not meanness or viciousness.

"I need some help, old-timer," Conagher said.

"My name's Colgrove," the crippled man snapped. "Dan Colgrove. And I'm not so old."

Conagher grinned. "The fire's not out, I can see that, except in that miniature stove you carry. I see you've got a walkin' stick there. That mean you could maybe walk me into town and let the friendly folks know they made a mistake?"

Dan Colgrove made his decision without hesitation. If there was even any serious doubt that a mistake had been made, he could do nothing else. "I can. I knew this whole affair meant nothing but trouble—"

The door burst open suddenly. Willa Colgrove stood in the opening, a rifle butted firmly against her shoulder, its muzzle pointing directly at the tall stranger's chest.

"You'll do nothing of the kind, Pa. Stay where you are!"

For the beat of several seconds no one spoke or moved. Then Willa stepped carefully onto the porch. The aim of her rifle did not waver.

Conagher glanced down at the crippled man in the rocking chair. "She belong to you?"

"She does. Willa, don't be a fool—"

"I'm not the one who's been taken in," she retorted.

"Hell, he's no killer," her father said impatiently. "If you were any judge of men at all, you'd know it. Now put that rifle down, and—"

"I'll do nothing of the kind. And if you move, mister, I'll shoot. Don't make the mistake of thinking I won't, or can't."

The tall man studied her for a long moment. Then he said, "I doubt you will."

"I warn you, I will—and I won't lose any sleep over it. Pa, you get out of the way. I don't like you being so close to him."

"He doesn't even know Bud Selvy," her father said angrily. "I tell you, Willa, this is the wrong man!"

"Because he told you so?" There was scorn in the girl's tone now. "That's not good enough. What else would he say? All I see is a man with a gun tied to his leg and blood all over him. You think he wouldn't say whatever he had to say to get a horse or whatever it is he wants?"

"Damn it, Willa—"

"It's my own blood," Conagher said quietly. "If that makes any difference."

Willa Colgrove checked a quick retort. For the first time, a flicker of something that might have been uncertainty appeared in her eyes. Conagher saw it, and at the same time saw the striking shading of those eyes, the violet color that was unlike anything he had seen before. He felt a strange shock run through him, as if in that instant he had suddenly become aware all at once of the fact that this creature holding a rifle against him was a beautiful young woman, tall and graceful and shining haired, with a fire of courage in her that he could only admire.

"You're a good talker," she said. "I suppose you're just as quick with that gun. But I wouldn't make the mistake of reaching for it."

"Wouldn't think of it," Conagher murmured.

"Willa, for God's sake will you listen to me for a minute?" Dan Colgrove demanded. "Before you hurt somebody?"

Her glance flicked toward him. "I know what I'm doing—"

Conagher moved with a swiftness that she wouldn't have believed possible an instant before. He had seemed exhausted, leaning his weight away from his wounded leg, a palm upraised and held out toward her in mild protest. Then he leaped toward her like a snake striking. His right arm lashed out and struck the barrel of the Winchester, knocking it upward as her finger squeezed the trigger. The shot went high.

The solid kick of the butt against her shoulder drove her back against the doorjamb. Then the tall man was close against her, pinning her there. His right hand had closed on the barrel and he wrenched it—with surprising ease, she would remember later—from her grasp.

His face was inches from hers. In that moment she was strongly conscious of the essential maleness of him, the strength and purpose, the unyielding hardness of his body, the smells of leather and horseflesh, of blood and sweat and something less definable. "I didn't think you'd do it," he said, in a tone that was oddly gentle.

Then he was crossing the porch in two long strides, taking her Winchester with him. She saw him look back once, and she saw him stumble, his left leg dragging, before he turned the corner of the house and was gone.

She heard shouts from the direction of the business district. A light appeared in another house nearby. Running figures materialized on the side street.

A sudden weakness attacked her legs, and she leaned trembling against the frame of the door. Her thoughts whirled in confusion, and from them unexpectedly one sentence the man had spoken leaped out clearly. *It's my own blood, if that makes any difference.*

She heard her father rise and struggle toward her, and she thought, *My God, what if it's true? What if he's the wrong man!*

SIX

From Harvey Parker's office in the Dust Cutter, Tug Walsh glanced through the open doorway at the barroom beyond. He could see Ralph Reese, grinning, hold up his right hand for a grizzled teamster to imitate as he was sworn in. When the swearing was done, the teamster guffawed. He dived immediately toward the glass waiting on the bar, poured in advance for each man willing to be deputized. Reese had his own full glass near his elbow.

Walsh scowled. He liked the way this night's work was shaping up even less than before. And he didn't think much of the posse Reese was assembling. What lay ahead was grim work for sober men, not a carnival for a bunch of reckless hotheads or footloose cowboys with two much whisky in their bellies.

He turned to find Bud Selvy watching him. Selvy wore a smile on his lips, but his blue eyes were coolly appraising.

"What do you think, Walsh?" Selvy asked.

"About what?"

"About what Ike has just been saying. Might be a good idea if we all paid attention." Selvy's smile seemed intended to dilute the sting from his words. "What do you think this Rorke means to do?"

"What he came here for," Tug Walsh answered bluntly. "He won't run. Way I understand it, if he don't kill you, Selvy, he don't get paid. And if he's the kind of man you say, he won't be scared off. A man like that, a hired gun, wouldn't be worth a bag of salt if he let himself be run off by a bunch of townies. He'd be finished, and he'd know that. Takin' a bullet like he done, hell, I figger that only makes it certain he'll stick. He's got to make somebody pay up for that."

"If?" Selvy murmured. "You have any doubts about what kind of man he is?"

The cattleman shifted his weight uneasily. He was not afraid of Selvy, as he guessed some members of the Reception Committee were. His uneasiness was centered on the man called Rorke. It caused him now to turn and close the door, shutting off the noise from the saloon. Coolidge and Isiah Howarth, who had been chosen as the first shift of bodyguards to stay with Selvy, watched him with the apprehensiveness that had been in their eyes ever since the killer's escape from the livery stables. Only Selvy seemed unperturbed.

It hadn't been so when the committee reached the saloon with news of Rorke's escape. Selvy's face had flushed red, dark as crushed cherries. In his livid rage he had turned on Ike Coolidge, who was unlucky enough to have spoken up first. "You fools let him get away? My God, how did you manage that? He rode right into your trap, didn't he?"

"Yes, but—"

"And not one of the six of you could shoot a man across that yard? It's a wonder you didn't hurt yourselves!"

"Now hold on, Selvy, there's no call to jump on us. It wasn't our fault—"

"Whose was it, then?" Selvy had banged his fist down so hard on Parker's desk that the inkwell jumped, spattering black drops across the mahogany. "God save me from volunteers!"

"Maybe you should have been there yourself," Tug Walsh had said. He had come to Selvy feeling as sheepish as the others, but the man's reaction had nettled him.

Bud Selvy had swung toward him with a fury in his eyes so naked that Walsh had felt a sharp chill, followed by a wary stiffening. "I stayed here because my friends talked me into it," Selvy had said harshly. "I numbered you among them, Walsh. Maybe I made a mistake about that, presumin' on bein' neighbors."

Tug Walsh had reddened with resentment, but he had checked his anger, warned by something in Selvy that had always been veiled behind his smiling manner. Some of that resentment still lingered in him now as he pondered his answer to Selvy's pointed question about the wounded gunman, and he felt a stubbornness rise.

"He don't act like he's such hell on wheels," Walsh said. "He could've killed Sanderson there in the stables, slit his throat without him makin' a sound, but he didn't. He just laid him out. And as near as I can figger, he didn't throw any lead our way at all. A real catamount like he's supposed to be should've left his mark on more than one of us." Walsh paused, disturbed by the direction of his own argument, not yet certain where it was leading him. "Looks like he didn't mean no harm to Dan or Willa Colgrove neither."

Bud Selvy eyed him without expression for a moment, but he had the veil up, even if he wasn't smiling, and the cattleman could not assess what was in this mind. *He's not what he seems,* Walsh thought.

Selvy said, "You're forgettin' a few things, it seems to me. You forget he was wounded there in the barn, and he might have panicked for a while, not knowin' how many of you there were. Besides, what he did was the smart thing. Instead of throwin' lead in the dark without hittin' anything, and lettin' you know where he was, he stayed quiet and he was able to slip the noose. That was smart, Walsh." Selvy's tension showed as he shoved back Harvey Parker's chair and rose to pace the crowded room, with his squat, powerful body resembling a bear in a cage. "I reckon it's nobody's fault he turned out so slick. I don't mean to say it was. He got out of that barn, and he put as much of the town between himself and the stables as he could. Then he moved in on the first likely lookin' place and grabbed himself a rifle. He didn't use it on old Dan, or Willa, thank God, but he didn't have time for that neither, after Willa squeezed the trigger of that Winchester to warn us." The burly man stopped abruptly, confronting Walsh. "Maybe he didn't show any of his claws yet, but I guarantee you he will. He didn't borrow that rifle to pound stakes with. He means to use it. You see it any other way, Walsh?"

"No," the cattleman admitted.

Selvy stared at him. A faint smile had reappeared, but it wasn't in his pale blue eyes. "I don't want any man takin' up my fight if he hasn't the heart for it." He nodded toward the closed door, as if he had made his own judgment of Walsh's reasons for wanting privacy. "That the way it is with you, Tug? You want to back out? If that's how it sizes up, there's no one gonna hold you down. Ain't that right, boys?" He glanced toward Howarth and Coolidge in turn, waiting for their quick nods, before he looked at Walsh again. "You just rode into this today, and I don't suppose anyone's gonna hold it against you if you want to ride right on out again."

He waited then, and Walsh saw that Howarth and Coolidge were also waiting. Both had been more nervous than he was at the stables, but they seemed to draw strength from Bud Selvy's presence. Tug Walsh realized that he had been neatly shoved and herded into a corner of the pen, and there was no way out but the one Selvy left him, the one that put him in the chute where Selvy wanted him to go.

"I didn't say that," Walsh growled uncomfortably. "Damn it, Selvy, all I'm sayin' is, we don't know much about this killer, not much at all."

"You'll know more than enough if he has his way."

Abruptly Selvy's manner changed. A broad grin broke out across his face. He stepped around a corner of the big desk and clapped a hand across Walsh's back. Selvy liked to put hands on a man in friendliness, and it was only when he did so that you realized how little like a town business-man he really was, how much power and strength there was in that burly body and the grip of his big hands.

"Hell, Tug, I know you're on my side all the way." Selvy chuckled, his eyes twinkling. "I know one way to smoke this heller out of the long grass. I could just parade with you boys down the center of town. That'd do it for sure!"

"You'll do no such thing!" Isiah Howarth said, bristling.

"No sirree," Ike Coolidge agreed. "You'll stay put right here. The posse will find him; don't you worry about that. Don't forget, he's hurting. He left a bucket of blood in the stables, like Walsh said, and there was more over at Col-grove's place. He can't stay on his feet very long that way."

Grudgingly Tug Walsh agreed. There was no sense at all in having Selvy step out where he could be felled by a single rifle shot fired from some dark alleyway. As long as the gunman was looking for Selvy, he would have to show himself. And he wouldn't be able to risk waiting for daylight to expose him.

But even as he nodded, Walsh sensed that he had been maneuvered, like the other members of the Reception Com-mittee, and he didn't enjoy the feeling. How far did the manipulation go? When had it begun?

In the end it didn't seem to make any difference. The killer was loose in the town, armed with a rifle and, ac-cording to Sanderson, twin six-guns. He was more danger-ous now than any four-legged animal crowded into a cor-ner. He had to be cut down, and there would be no time to ask questions.

Tug Walsh would go out into the street with Reese and his ragged posse, not liking any part of it but knowing that he was almost as jittery as anyone else on the Reception Committee or among its newly deputized vigilantes. And if he came face to face with the stranger called Rorke, he would shoot first and fast, and hope to God he was quick enough.

"We'll handle him," Walsh said flatly. His glance flicked over Ike Coolidge and Isiah Howarth. "You do your job, and that's to make sure nobody gets through that door standin' up." His gaze touched Selvy once more as he opened the door and looked back. "That's what the committee agreed on, and that's the way it'll be. But if Rorke ever gets this far, God help us all!"

SEVEN

Except for the searchers occasionally calling out to each other, the town of Bitter Creek was unnaturally quiet. Owen Conagher guessed that most of the town's respectable citizens had long ago pulled their children indoors and locked their doors. Although the night was still young, few lights showed in the scattered houses, and most of the businesses along the main street were boarded up and dark.

Most of the settlers in a town like this shunned violence, Conagher thought. Bitter Creek was a cow town with an air of permanence. Its citizens were not boom-town people, the prospectors, get-rich-quick schemers, gamblers, thieves, and drifters who made up the average population of a brawling frontier settlement. In his brief flight through the back yards and alleys of the town, Conagher had caught glimpses of a steepled church, a Masonic Lodge meeting hall over a store, a one-room schoolhouse on a little knoll south of the business district, a score or more of painted houses with fences around neatly tended gardens and yards, which more than outbalanced the few decrepit shacks at one end of town near the freight yard.

A pretty, respectable, growing town, filling up with people who went to church on Sundays and shunned anything more dangerous than a Saturday-night cowpuncher on the prod.

All of which made Conagher's reception at the livery stables more remarkable, for he was now convinced that the excitable, wild-shooting ambushers were some of those law-abiding, "respectable" people—a fact to which he probably owed his life. A meaner bunch would have had what was left of him rolled in a blanket for morning planting in the town's Boot Hill.

Conagher tensed. Someone spoke, and the voice was closer than he had anticipated.

"Watch out for that alley, Luke. He could be in there."

"If'n he is, I'll chew him up and spit out the pieces." The boastful declaration was slurred, as if the speaker had been priming himself too long at the Dust Cutter.

Conagher heard the scuff of dragging footsteps, then the crash of something overturned. He felt his body flinch from the sound, and a muscle jumped in his cheek.

The line of searchers was drawing close. He had to make another run soon. He was slowly being pushed back through the town, retreating westward toward the livery stables at the far end. Whoever had organized the hunt was being methodical and careful.

"Stick together!" a heavier voice than the first two barked. "Damn it, I told you not to go it alone. He'll jump one man a lot quicker than two together." The warning carried a weight of natural authority. The voice was that of a man who, if he was not a designated leader, was nevertheless the kind who tended to command respect, perhaps because he was steadier than most in a crisis.

Owen Conagher crouched in a narrow slot between two buildings near the center of town. He was in the deep shadows next to some boxes that filled up part of the passageway. He felt heavy-limbed, and he was reluctant to move. He was like a man freezing in deep snow, wanting only to go to sleep, and he recognized the danger of the feeling, the gathering weakness it warned of. He had lost a lot of blood.

Earlier, running from the Colgrove house with the girl's rifle, he had had to make a hard choice. He could have lit a shuck for the foothills to the south, losing himself quickly in the folds and fissures of the landscape, with little worry about being found while it was dark. The hazard was that he would have been on foot. He couldn't travel far or fast with a game leg, and he would have left a plain track for any posse to follow in the morning. He had also considered taking refuge in the schoolhouse, but he had rejected that possibility because the building was too isolated on its knoll. If he had been found there, he would have been trapped. A dozen men could easily surround the place. Finally he had decided to hide in the town itself.

At the time, his reasoning had seemed sound enough. He was the wrong man, being shot at for the wrong reasons. Somewhere in the town was a man who knew it. He had learned that much from Dan and Willa Colgrove. The vigilantes at the livery stables had been waiting for the arrival of a hired gun, a killer expected about the time Conagher showed up. And the man that killer was looking for called himself Bud Selvy.

All Conagher had to do was find this Selvy and show himself to him before the vigilantes found him.

This argument had quieted a more sober and sensible voice in his mind. The truth was that he wouldn't run. There was in him a stubborn anger, a determination to show up these hair-trigger townsfolk and to fling their mistake in their faces. That mixture of pride and anger overrode common sense, as it generally did.

He had seen some of the searchers leave the saloon and fan out toward the east end of town, where a line had been organized. That line was moving slowly westward, sweeping the town, searching every alley and store, knocking at the door of every house.

Now the line was pulling close, and Conagher crept away from his cover toward the rear of the two buildings that hemmed him in. The moon had risen, and when it emerged from behind some drifting cloud cover, as it did now, the main street seemed as bright as day. Conagher wanted no part of that street.

"I think I heard somethin'," a voice said.

Conagher froze. Cold fingered the back of his neck. The speaker was directly behind him, and he sounded no more than spitting distance away.

He saw that he had waited too long, underestimating the eagerness of some of these hunters.

"Aw, hell, you'd hear angels singin' in hell," a rougher voice jeered.

"He's close, I tell you—I heard him."

"Well, I don't hear nothin'."

"Damn it, *listen!*"

Conagher did not move. He breathed shallowly through his open mouth, and he refrained from even a shift of weight that might draw a rub of leather. He had let himself be trapped. All those two waddies had to do was take a couple of steps closer and they would be blocking the exit of this passageway. And from the street end came the thump of boots on the boardwalk, the signal of someone calling across the street to another searcher.

"Nothin'," the deep voice growled, "I told ya; he ain't even in this town no more. Hell, when he lit out from Colgrove's place, he was clear. Why would he come back here where he'd be sure to git caught?"

"Maybe." The sharp-eared hunter seemed disappointed. "Hell, I was lookin' to have some fun."

"Well, you ain't gonna find none here. I tell you . . ." The voice lowered to a conspiratorial pitch. "Look what I brung along."

"Where'd you git that?" Sharp ears demanded. "Walsh said no drinkin' outside."

"Sneaked it off the bar when that Reese was so busy puffin' hisself up. What say we just hold up this search for a spell and finish this off 'fore I drop it or some of that gold spills out."

"Not here, you nitwit!" his companion urged. "What if Walsh jumps us?"

"Who the hell is Walsh? I don't curl up every time he makes a noise."

"You're swore in, just like me." The voice faded suddenly as the two men turned away. "Come along. I know where we can sit out a few minutes . . ."

Owen Conagher waited until the voices and the accompanying scrape of footsteps moved out of earshot. Then he eased back on his heels, drawing a deeper breath. Close, he thought. It was a long time since he'd shaved it that fine.

And he was still in trouble. The main line of searchers was all around him now, and some of them might not be so careless about a dark patch.

A door banged and an "All clear!" sang out. Conagher glanced over his shoulder toward the moonlit street. He couldn't go that way, and the back alley was suspect. He couldn't be sure how far those two saloon recruits had gone, or how close others might be.

Hastily he examined the pile of empty crates. They looked flimsy, and the stack had been carelessly piled up. Would they hold him?

He examined the roof line overhead. The back section of the building to his right was an extension, a kind of lean-to with a slanting tin roof that was little more than six feet from the ground at the back edge. Where Conagher crouched behind the stack of crates, the roof was within his reach.

He decided against jumping for it. That way, he was certain to make too much noise. All he needed was one step up.

Gingerly he tested one of the larger boxes. It seemed fairly solid. Another boot scuffed the boardwalk near the far end of his passageway and Conagher knew that he couldn't wait any longer. He'd had all the luck he could count on for one night during the shooting at the livery stables.

He stepped onto the crate and reached for the edge of the lean-to's roof. The box quivered under his weight. He slid Willa Colgrove's Winchester onto the roof ahead of him. As he got an elbow over the edge and pushed up, there was a sudden, sharp crack. The frame of the light-weight box snapped. The crate skidded to one side, and another tumbled down as support was removed. In an instant the whole pile was spilling with a crash that roared in Conagher's ears as loud as an avalanche.

He hauled himself onto the tin roof and rolled away from the edge as shouts rang out. A last box tilted and fell, and two quick shots boomed in the darkness of the passage.

"Over here!" someone yelled. Others took up the cry. Footsteps pounded toward Conagher from every direction.

He knew that it was only a matter of seconds before someone figured out what had happened and lifted up to scan the low roof of the lean-to. He rolled toward the back edge, hung breathlessly near it as someone ran by just below him. Then he took another turn and dropped over the edge.

A ragged tip of the tin roof raked across his bad leg, digging into his flesh and tearing as he fell. That raw wound seemed to catch every sharp edge. Conagher landed on his feet, staggered, caught his balance, and bolted.

He ran head-on into another man turning the corner of the building, coming up to cut him off. The impact stopped both men in their tracks. The searcher was too startled or stunned to cry out immediately, and for a second he confronted Conagher in the shadows. Then he opened his mouth and Conagher hit him with a wild swing of the Winchester that caught a fistful of teeth. The man went down as if he had run into a rope.

Conagher jumped past him. He turned the next corner as another gunshot blazed behind him.

The heady aroma of garbage enveloped him as he stumbled past another building. He slipped and skated precariously over an area of spillage near some loaded barrels. Then a board fence six feet high loomed ahead, and of a sudden he felt leaden and weak, doubting that he could ever scale it.

The confused, excited shouting behind him spurred him on. After fleeting hesitation, he tossed the borrowed rifle over the fence and tried to follow it. He jumped up and dragged himself to the top. There he felt all the strength drain out of his arms. He hung for several heartbeats, silhouetted darkly against the sky. As he began to slip back, he heard a shrill yell. A bullet whacked into the board above him as he tumbled to the ground.

Conagher scrambled along the base of the fence until he reached the platform behind the restaurant which supplied the garbage whose overripe smells filled the night. He moved now in despair, for he was certainly trapped, but desperation drove him toward the only available cover. An oversized rat skittered away from him as he crawled into a large garbage bin, one of two along the left side of the platform. He was immediately part of a slick, crumbling, greasy pile that made his flesh crawl and his belly heave threateningly.

It was a hell of a place to die, he thought. His right hand dragged his Colt clear as footsteps pounded closer and shouts chased one another like sparks.

"Over here!"

"Look out, Jimmy—he's cornered!"

"Circle that yard. You, Luke, and Willy—head him off if he tries to duck south."

"I saw him go over the fence!"

Conagher heard them tightening the circle around him, and he felt a rush of the wild, unreasoning anger which had first come to him in the livery stables. He didn't mind cashing out so much. What outraged him was knowing that it was all a foolish mistake, for which these good citizens would hold their hats and mumble apologies over his grave.

Then one of them ran past him—less than five feet away.

"Hold up, here's where he went over when I seen him. There's his blood. Walsh? He's over there, I tell you!"

Conagher felt something crawl over his cheek and he gagged. His thoughts were sluggish now, and he was slow to comprehend what was happening. He waited for one of the hunters to turn toward the bins on the restaurant platform, but none did. From where he lay, facing out, he saw two or three other men run by. He heard the one called Walsh directing some others as they surrounded the fenced yard Conagher had tried to enter.

A moment later came the crash of a gate bursting open, and the slam of a six-shooter hammering off two quick shots.

Then silence.

When the querulous questioning started, Owen Conagher managed a grin. By then he realized that they had bypassed him in their hurry. Whoever had seen him skylined across the top of the fence had assumed that he had dropped on the far side. He had left his blood on the boards to confirm the assumption, as well as the rifle he had thrown ahead.

Someone stomped toward him. Conagher's finger tightened on the trigger of his Colt. Then the posse member turned aside to funnel along the passage next to the restaurant that led toward the business street. An angry voice berated another searcher for letting the wounded killer slip past him, and the man accused protested in an aggrieved tone.

In spite of an overpowering urge to dig out of the crawling pile of garbage in which he lay, Conagher held still until the vigilantes gave up their search in the nearby yard and began to spread out once more into a long line, one grumbling, another expressing his bafflement aloud, still a third insisting that he *had* seen the gunman as he went over the fence.

A rat ran across Conagher's leg. It stopped in the sudden way of such varmints, staring at him boldly. Conagher glared back and took aim with his Colt. *If you don't move on, I'll have me some target practice.* As if he had understood, the rat darted away, vanishing around a corner of the bin.

When he was sure that the line had moved far enough away, Conagher crawled out of the garbage bin onto the open platform, gulping at the fresher air. He found his left hand alive with maggots, as thick as a white glove. In revulsion he pawed most of them away. He rolled off the platform onto a patch of grass, where he wiped his hands clean and tried to brush away whatever still clung or crawled over his clothes.

It came to him that he was temporarily safe. The search was moving through the town in a sweeping line, and he was now behind the line, in the section cleared.

Yet he waited a full minute before he left the shadows of the platform. Whoever was directing that methodical search might have been shrewd enough to leave a trailing guard or two. Only when he judged that this precaution had been neglected did Conagher limp away from the restaurant, turning once more toward the east side of the town.

He carried the stomach-turning stench of the garbage pit with him. If the posse turned back, he thought, they wouldn't have to see him this time. They could just follow the smell.

He knew that he had to clean himself up, especially his open wounds. The one in his leg, opened and widened when he went over the ragged edge of the tin roof, was bleeding anew. He also needed rest, for he was stumbling and reeling sometimes, and he had to fight off dizzying blackness. But how could he rest? The searchers would not give up until they had found him. Believing what they did, that a cat-eyed killer was among them, hurt and raging, they wouldn't dare close their eyes in sleep until he was found.

Conagher had to find a hole, one where he could hide until daylight. But if he didn't clean up that leg first, it might not matter what else happened. Conagher had had experience enough of neglected cuts and wounds to know that this one could not be ignored, even if it stopped bleeding the strength out of him.

At the side street Conagher halted. Instead of crossing the open space, he clung to the shadowed side of the corner building, moving under the protection of a side staircase until he neared the edge of the boardwalk. When he heard no sound of movement along the walk or street, he eased forward until he could peer around the corner.

Along the business street some half a dozen buildings showed lights. Most prominent was the Dust Cutter, a busy place this night, with lights showing upstairs as well as down. Across the intersection on the opposite corner was the hotel. As Conagher watched, someone appeared in the doorway and stepped out onto the veranda to gaze along the street toward the retreating line of vigilantes. Other figures were visible in the lobby, and a shadow moved in front of a lamp before an upstairs window.

The whole town was not engaged in hunting him down, Conagher reflected. But the town would breathe easier when the quarry had been flushed and brought down.

As he turned his head, his eye caught the neatly lettered sign, gilt letters over black, mounted on the wall at the foot of the stairway: DR. RAYMOND HALL, Medical Practitioner.

A faint hope started Conagher up the stairs. There seemed to be a hundred of them, and their numbers and steepness increased as he plodded slowly upward. When he reached the top he was surprised to find himself sinking to his knees. You wouldn't have figured a little scratch under the ribs or a bullet in the leg would take so much of the sap out, he thought, bemused.

He found the door to the doctor's office. It was locked.

A narrow platform led toward the front of the building. Conagher crept along it on hands and knees. Before he reached the end of the platform facing the street, he felt another attack of dizziness. He lay flat, waiting for the night to stop whirling. He had the sensation of clinging to a slowly spinning top, and when it began to lose speed, it tilted over and he slid off into darkness . . .

Conagher woke to a lurching panic. The feeling of hanging on to a tilted surface was still with him, and it was a minute before he realized that he was lying on the level platform at the top of the stairs of the corner building overlooking Bitter Creek's main intersection.

He wondered how long he had been unconscious. Seconds? Minutes? An hour?

Pushing up to set his back against the wall of the building, he felt one hand slide over a dark slickness on the platform where he had lain. His own blood. It was neither dry nor sticky. He hadn't been there long.

The sickening smells of the garbage pit assaulted his nostrils. He had to get out of these clothes and cleanse his wounds, for his own peace of mind as well as to avoid sending up a signal to the vigilantes. The need was a lot clearer than any plan that would make it possible.

The problem reminded him suddenly of Big Red, who carried Conagher's few belongings in his saddlebags and blanket roll. How had the horse fared in the shooting at the stables? Well enough, Conagher hoped. Red bolted when Conagher jumped off, but there had been no scream of terror to suggest that he had been hit.

Returning anger flooded new strength into his arms, enabling him to push himself to his feet. He had slipped through the line of vigilantes once, but they would be beating the brush again when their search through the other end of town came up empty. Conagher had to use the few minutes open to him to find the man called Selvy and prove that he wasn't Selvy's hired killer.

And he had discovered something from his brief survey of the business district. Selvy's Mercantile was in the middle of the block across the way, nearly opposite the Dust Cutter. It was a wide, frame, two-story building, larger than anything else in the street except the hotel and the saloon. The building had been dark, and unless the proprietor lived in back, it didn't seem likely that Selvy would be there at this hour. On the other hand, it was equally improbable that he was at home with his family, if he had one, indifferent to the activities in town that were being carried out in his behalf.

Where would he be? In the hotel? In the saloon, which seemed to be headquarters for the vigilantes? Out in the street with the hunters?

Or, perhaps, holed up in his own store, close to everything, but keeping out of sight until word came that his would-be killer had been dealt with as he deserved?

It was worth checking out, Conagher decided. He turned back toward the stairs.

Footsteps approaching the intersection along the boardwalk froze Conagher at the top step. There were two men, and they were in a hurry. At the side street they pulled up, looking around. Conagher couldn't risk moving. At that moment the tattered clouds covering the moon began to edge away from the white sphere, like a lid opening slowly over a sightless eye. Conagher was caught in the full glow of the moon. If either of the men below him glanced his way, or even if one of those on the hotel veranda across the way looked up, he would be seen.

"How the hell could he have got behind us?" one of the men at the edge of the boardwalk asked skeptically.

"I got a feeling," the other replied in a heavy, thought-ful tone that was familiar.

"Hell, Walsh, they's gonna flush him out the other way and we'll miss out on the fun!"

Walsh grunted. "That what you think this is? If they do flush him, I got a hunch you'll be glad you wasn't there when it happened."

"He's supposed to be such a heller, how come he runs so fast?"

Walsh didn't answer. He was the one to worry about, Conagher thought.

On the other hand, Walsh sounded levelheaded and calm enough to listen to reason if Conagher could just get to him before he drew iron. The possibility was tempting, but this night's events had made Conagher cautious. He wasn't going to jump until he was sure.

"We'll circle back this way," Walsh said. "If he slipped through the line, maybe we can pinch him in between us."

"Hell, Walsh, if he's there, he could jump us easy," the other man grumbled, less eager to find the wounded gun-man when he wasn't running with a pack.

"I'll go first," Walsh retorted. "I won't be lookin' be-hind me, but you damned well better be there."

Conagher hugged the wall at the top of the staircase. He glanced toward the moon in the hope of more cloud cover. None seemed close, although heavy black clouds had been gathering over the mountains to the west. The men below him stepped out of shadow into the moon-bathed road. They approached the alleyway cautiously, not looking back —or up. Conagher wondered how they could fail to hear the drumbeat of his heart.

Once more he glanced skyward, this time not scanning the night sky but inspecting the roof line immediately above. Before the pair below turned back, he had to be off this platform and out of sight. He could no longer risk going down the stairs or trying to reach the mercantile across the street.

He realized also that there was not much run left in him.

Walsh, the leader of the two vigilantes, a heavy-set man with a cowman's rolling walk, stepped out of sight around the corner. The other waddy hesitated. When he followed Walsh into the alley, Conagher rose. Quickly he stepped onto the porch railing and reached for the flat roof. Desperation gave him the surge of strength that carried him over the top with surprising speed.

He lay prone, listening. No alarm sounded.

Conagher rose and, keeping low, slipped across the roof. The adjoining building butted directly against the first one. It was a story lower. He glanced toward the alley, but he could neither see nor hear the searchers. Silently he lowered himself over the edge, feeling a painful pull at his side as he hung suspended. Then he dropped.

His leg gave way and he sprawled on the lower roof.

He did not know how long he lay there. He was certain that he had made too much noise and that he couldn't linger, but it required an enormous effort of will to drag himself up and stumble across the roof. At least he had placed a barrier between himself and the side street, but he wanted to be farther from that busy hotel on the corner across the way.

He stopped at the roof's edge. A passage loomed between this building and the next one. It was hardly more than three feet wide, but it seemed to Owen Conagher like a long jump.

Yet it was one he had to make. That next building was his goal—the saloon.

The Dust Cutter was two stories high. A full balcony fronted the building and continued along the east wall facing Conagher. The roof overhang left the balcony in shadow. There were a number of small windows along this wall, suggesting a series of rooms with access from the balcony. Moreover, there was a door at the far end. Lights glowed behind several of the windows, and voices filtered up to Conagher from the saloon.

The saloon offered hope. If the search for him was being directed from here, somewhere inside he might find a cooler head, a chance to tell his story without catching a bullet first. Or, among its many rooms, a place to hide under cover until the moon waned or those storm clouds moved in from the mountains. At any rate it seemed to offer more promise than an open roof or savage pursuit through the back yards of Bitter Creek . . . and the vigilantes would not expect him under the very roof from which so many had set out to find him.

The Dust Cutter's balcony was perhaps a step higher than the roof of the smaller building. Conagher had to jump for the railing across the gap. He chose a spot where there was a supporting post to grab. He didn't look down at the canyon below. If he fell, he would learn how deep it was and how hard the ground.

Conagher stepped to the edge, crouched and sprang. He caught hold of the post and locked both arms around it. His long body swung inward in a hard, swiveling arc. As his left leg crashed into the railing, pain exploded through him. The shock loosened his grip on the post. He slipped downward.

His right arm, looped around the post, slammed into the railing and brought him up short, saving a crippling plunge to the path below. He hooked his elbow over the top rail and hung there, unable to move.

For what seemed like a full minute, Conagher hung from the railing, his body swaying, while wave after wave of pain went through his body. When first he tried to drag himself over the railing to the safety of the balcony, his leaden arms lacked the strength. Shaking his head in wonderment, Conagher managed to get one boot over the balcony's edge. It gave him enough leverage to heave himself upward and he fell over the railing into the shadows.

A crushing weight tried to push him through the floor. He hauled himself to his feet in spite of it, still shaking his head in surprise at his weakness. It was not something you could get used to or accept as normal. You kept expecting your arms and legs to respond as they always had. A small piece of lead wasn't so much weight to carry.

Conagher knew that he was no longer thinking clearly, and that he had to find a hole to crawl into for a spell. Glancing along the balcony, he chose one of the dark windows. It was open a few inches to admit the evening breeze, and he shoved it upward.

He had his head and shoulders through the opening when a door on the far side of the room opened.

A young woman—in the dimness she seemed young to Owen Conagher's wavering vision—stood rooted in the doorway, gaping at him. Neither she nor Conagher moved.

"Don't yell," he mumbled.

"Who are you?" she demanded. Then, her voice sharpening, "You could come in the right way. Or were you lookin' for something free?"

Conagher shook his head. He dragged his left leg across the windowsill and sagged against the wall. "You've got it wrong. I was just . . ."

The words eluded him. He wanted to explain but the effort didn't seem worthwhile. He stared mutely at the woman. From the light that filtered past her into the room, he was able to see a rumpled bed, an open wardrobe in which some frilly pink and green and scarlet garments hung, a washstand holding a large white bowl and pitcher. He saw a frown crease the woman's forehead. He was aware of long, auburn hair hanging free, of an expanse of billowing pink flesh and green velvet, and he thought, *She's not so young as you figured.*

Then he felt himself falling.

A braided rug on the floor cushioned his fall. His cheek was digging into it when the door where the woman had been standing suddenly closed, shutting off the light. Welcome darkness closed round him, and with a sigh Conagher let himself go, as if he were releasing a physical hold on reality. The darkness spun around him, slowly at first, then faster and faster, like the waters of a deep whirlpool, sucking him toward the center and finally spinning him helplessly into the black core.

EIGHT

An explosion of gunfire and a shrill yelp brought Tug Walsh on the run to the alleyway behind Ike Coolidge's bank. There he found a drunken cowhand—a no-account named Rankin whom he had taken on for his spring roundup and let go as soon as he could fairly do so—bitterly complaining, while another man, a rough teamster who worked for Selvy's Freight Line, guffawed. Quinn, the teamster, had taken a shot at Rankin and the bullet had come close enough to take a bite out of Rankin's hat brim. Quinn thought it was a hell of a joke, and he was doubled over laughing, rocking on his heels.

Walsh turned away in disgust. The entire hunt, not to mention the Reception Committee itself, was becoming a joke, one with the potential of turning as vicious and dangerous as Quinn's reckless shot.

For a while the cattleman had been able to keep some order in the search. He had led one sweep through the town, Reese another, followed by a wide circle that extended to the creek west and north of town and to Boot Hill to the south. Only the plain eastward, as flat as a billiard table, had been omitted. Even at night it offered little concealment for a hundred yards or more. Beyond that circle, the man they hunted could be anywhere, and Walsh had called off any futile tracking into the foothills.

Weary, angry, footsore, and hungry, Tug Walsh was more than half-convinced the fugitive had fled. He hoped so.

One reason for his hope was that he knew the search was

disintegrating. The number of men deputized had increased each hour, every man of them swearing in after being cajoled and prodded by a few free drinks in Harvey
Parker's barroom, with the promise of more to follow the
end of a successful hunt. There were too many now to keep
track of. A few, tough teamsters and drifters and no-ac-
counts like Rankin, were troublemakers who could not be
controlled for long in a situation as disorganized as the
hunt was becoming.

All it took was a few, Tug Walsh knew, like a few nervous beeves starting a stampede.

Reaching the boardwalk, Walsh turned toward the saloon. He found himself wondering about Selvy and Harvey
Parker. The latter was known to be tightfisted enough to
squeeze a gold piece into foil. It wasn't like him to be passing out much free whisky, even out of friendship for one
of the town's up-and-coming citizens. Which meant that
Selvy was doing the buying . . . or that Selvy had a say in
what the Dust Cutter dispensed.

Hell, the man was like an octopus, Tug Walsh thought.
He had taken over Colgrove's freight line not long after
surfacing to buy the mercantile. Some said he had bailed
Sanderson out of trouble for a price. He had grabbed up
the section of land south of Walsh's Split-W spread—land
that Walsh himself had hoped one day to buy. And the
Dust Cutter as well? Had Parker lost too heavily at his own
tables, or, more likely, at some of the others in distant
towns where he was known to go on gambling sprees?

Walsh shook off the speculation. What mattered now
was that the hunt for the hired gunman was getting out of
hand. It had to be brought under rein . . . or stopped.

Walsh found Ike Coolidge and Isiah Howarth in earnest
conversation at a table in the Dust Cutter. The two had
been relieved of sentry duty outside Harvey Parker's office, where Selvy was still holed up, an hour before, and
they didn't seem to know what to do with themselves. Their

committee had got away from them; the swelling posse was out of their control. Ralph Reese, whom they had merely tolerated as a member of the Reception Committee because of his badge, had laughed at Ike Coolidge in open derision when the banker remonstrated with him. "He's drunk," Coolidge complained. "Surely you can see he's in no condition to lead a posse, Walsh."

Walsh, who didn't see exactly what could be done about the deputy as long as he wasn't falling down drunk, agreed that it was time to have another talk with Selvy before some of the townspeople were hurt. But as he turned toward Parker's office with the others, who seemed genuinely relieved by his response, he felt a tightening in his gut. He knew that Bud Selvy would not listen. The Reception Committee was supposed to have been someone else's idea, one that Selvy had accepted reluctantly, but what was happening now in the streets and alleys of the town was Selvy's doing.

The three members of the Reception Committee were near the office door when a man in dusty cowhand's garb stumbled out of the barroom onto the boardwalk. He reeled in a full circle, and Walsh saw, before the swinging doors closed, that he had his gun in his hand. A rift in the thickening cloud cover let the moon show through, and the cowpuncher yipped with delight. His six-gun lifted and in a few seconds, as fast as he could fumble off the shots, he had ventilated the offending night lamp. As if to confirm his success, the clouds moved over the moon's face once more, dousing the light, and Walsh heard the curly wolf's howl of triumph.

Isiah Howarth swore aloud, and Ike Coolidge muttered agreement. "It's coming to trouble," the banker said. "It has to stop."

One of Harvey Parker's idle card dealers was sharing sentry duty with a town loafer Tug Walsh vaguely recognized. The latter waved them into the office with a lop-sided grin.

They found Bud Selvy closeted with Harvey Parker. The saloonkeeper looked pallid—he was not in good health and was known to cough a lot. And Walsh noted that it was Selvy, not Parker, who sat in the big, comfortable leather chair behind the massive desk. With the two men, pale and sullen on the battered leather couch at one side of the room, was Dick Sanderson.

After inquiring about Sanderson's condition—he seemed to have nothing worse than a lump on his head and a frayed temper—Walsh gave a terse account of the frustrated search for the wounded gunfighter. He concluded with a caustic description of the worsening conditions in the street. "Trouble's building," the cattleman finished.

"We had trouble to begin with." Eyes twinkling, Selvy seemed to find the antics of some of the vigilantes amusing.

"We have more now."

"What do you want me to do?"

"Well, you can turn off the whisky tap for a start. I'd as soon turn a bunch of drunken Apaches loose as some of those you got out there now."

"Walsh is right," Howarth agreed crisply. "They've already broken into Ballard's place, and God knows what kind of stealing and looting is going on. If we don't put a halt to it soon—"

"That don't hardly seem a fair way to state it," Selvy protested. "Hell, those boys have to search every place in town. Damn it, that killer is here somewhere!"

"I don't think so," Walsh cut in. "I think he's cleared out. We'd have turned him up before this if he was still here."

"Maybe. Maybe you're even willing to take that chance. But it isn't your hide he wants to put holes in, is it?" Selvy asked pointedly. "I reckon what you're sayin', Walsh, is that you don't mind me takin' a chance on gettin' punctured."

"Looks to me like you're not runnin' much of a risk settin' behind that desk!"

The twinkle vanished abruptly from Selvy's blue eyes, leaving two hard bits of opaque color like flecks of turquoise. "You make it sound like all this was my idea," he said. "That includes swearin' in a posse to help out. Seems like you're all findin' it easy to forget I would've been clear over in the next county by now if I hadn't been talked out of it. Anyways, I don't see harm in Harvey here offerin' to buy a few drinks for the volunteers. I think you're worryin' too much about those boys. After all, they're only doin' what the Reception Committee couldn't handle. Isn't that about the size of it?"

"Hold on, Selvy," Coolidge objected. "That isn't exactly fair—"

"It's no worse than the way you were takin' up against the posse," Selvy pointed out. He mollified his tone and showed his teeth in a smile when he spoke to the banker, but his eyes remained cold. "You turnin' against me, too, Ike? Sounds like the committee must've had a meetin' I didn't know about." He swung toward Sanderson. "Was you in on it, Dick? Do you go along with the rest of the committee that I've been busy stirrin' up trouble?"

Sanderson glared sullenly at the three standing members of the committee. Walsh suddenly discovered that he was holding his hat, his calloused hands absently rolling the brim. The hands went still as he scowled, catching a picture that reminded him of going in, hat in hand, to face an angry range boss. Setting his jaw, he jammed the shapeless hat back on his head.

"I'm for diggin' that bastard out of his hole wherever he is," Sanderson said bitterly. "And I don't much care how it's done."

"Or who else gets hurt?" Walsh asked quietly.

"I'm the one nearly got his head cracked open!"

"Well, now, leastwise it isn't unanimous against me," Selvy said. He continued to smile, but a curl of contempt appeared at the corners of his mouth—or what seemed to Walsh like contempt. "What I'd say is, those that hasn't the stomach for finishin' what they started should back out right now, and go on home."

Ike Coolidge flushed. "You weren't so anxious to have us in our homes when this thing started."

"That's true enough," Selvy answered easily. "You boys tried to help me out, and I appreciate it. The way it stacks up, though, you weren't quite up to the job, and I'm not blamin' anyone for that. This Rorke is slick and he's smart and he's dangerous. I think now he has to be handled another way. Reese goes along with me, and he's made it all legal by deputizin' the volunteers. The way I see it, the best way to end this is to comb every foot of this town sideways and up until we find that hardcase killer. And that takes men—all the men we can find!"

"I'll have no part of it," Isiah Howarth snapped, his back up.

"Then you don't have to, Isiah," Selvy answered with an indifferent shrug. "Nobody's got you tied down. You'll find the door right behind you."

It was a direct challenge, and it said clearly that Selvy no longer needed the Reception Committee. Their earlier participation had already served to give sanction to what was being done, and nothing could change that. Howarth quickly saw his position and looked around for support.

Before anyone else could speak up, Selvy threw the challenge at Ike Coolidge. "You feel the same, Ike?"

Tug Walsh could see the conflict in the banker's eyes, his fear of the drunken mob measured against another kind of potential loss. Walsh wondered if anyone else in Bitter Creek knew as much as Coolidge about Selvy's growing power in the town. He watched the banker struggle with himself—and saw him cave in.

"I didn't exactly say that, Selvy. But like Walsh says, if this man has already escaped, what can be gained by letting that mob run wild outside? We're just asking for trouble!"

"Maybe. And it might be I can think of a way to handle that if you'll all go along with me. How about it, Walsh? Are you still game to finish what we started?"

It was, finally, the right thing to ask. Selvy's demand not only called the cattleman's courage into question, it also reminded him of his pledge when he joined the Reception Committee. However reluctantly he had made his promise, whatever misgivings he might have now, Walsh would see it through, as Selvy had shrewdly judged.

Even as he nodded, Tug Walsh saw the satisfaction in Bud Selvy's eyes. He didn't like what he saw. He would remember it, and it would temper any dealings he had in the future with Selvy—but it would not affect what had to be done this night.

"I've said my piece," Walsh said. "I didn't say we should give it up."

"Good. Well, now, it looks like we've still got a committee, and we all want the same thing." He grinned almost boyishly. "No hard feelings, Isiah?"

Red-faced, Howarth could only agree grudgingly to go along, not wanting to walk out on the committee alone. Once more Bud Selvy had had his way. But this time he had harmed himself, Tug Walsh thought. He was losing friends while winning the hand.

Now Selvy inquired about Alfred Williams, the missing member of the committee. Coolidge reported that he had seen Williams return to his shop after his hour of sentry duty. Grinning, Selvy suggested that the little Englishman had found the riotous ways of Texas a sight rougher than he had anticipated, and was now in full retreat, carrying

his fancy rifle with him, about as much use in a fight as
those redcoats Andy Jackson routed at New Orleans. "I
wouldn't be surprised if he was to keep right on runnin'
all the way back across the ocean—without gettin' his feet
wet!" Selvy joked.

The sally was spoken with a broad show of humor, but
Tug Walsh found it mean-spirited and vicious. Selvy, he
guessed, would discover a way to take his revenge against
anyone failing to support him all the way. That included
Isiah Howarth as well as Williams—and Walsh himself.

"All right, boys," Selvy said then, standing up and coming around the desk. "Come along—I've got a little surprise for you. I think I know how to make this fire-
breathin' posse tend to business."

Selvy led the way from the office into the barroom, leaving the members of the Reception Committee to follow
curiously. There were still a dozen men in the saloon,
along with a few of Harvey Parker's ladies. Others within
earshot on the boardwalk outside came in when Selvy
raised his voice to quiet the hubbub in the barroom.

"Give a listen, boys! You all know what's goin on here
tonight, I reckon. There's a hired gunman sneakin' around
out there somewhere. We know he's swallowed at least one
lead pill that didn't go down easy, but he's given us the slip
up till now. The sooner he's found, the sooner we can all
celebrate. So I'm postin' a reward, five hundred dollars in
gold, to the man who cuts him down, any way he can!"

There was a roar of approval from the well-primed lis-
teners, and within seconds, a stampede through the swinging doors to the street. Selvy swung around, grinning, to
face the startled members of the Reception Committee.
"There it is, gentlemen. Anyone wants to get in on the
winnings, I'm not gonna insist you stand duty outside my
door. I reckon a couple of Parker's boys can do that job."

"Do you think that was wise, Selvy?" Coolidge asked
nervously.

Selvy slapped him on the shoulder. "It'll get the job done, Ike. You saw them. If I've learned any one thing in my life, it's that a man will do most anythin' he wouldn't ordinarily do, and work harder at it, if he thinks there's gold where he's diggin'. You'll see. Within an hour I'll have that killer's scalp hangin' from a pole!"

He spoke with such ebullient confidence that the weary members of the committee could not help taking heart, in spite of their misgivings of a few moments earlier. Tug Walsh, however, continued to stare at Selvy suspiciously as the others fell into eager discussion of the surprising reward offer. He saw Selvy's glance flick toward the street. It was an unguarded moment, and Walsh saw something unexpected—an uneasy narrowing of Selvy's eyes that failed to hide the dark shadow of worry.

NINE

A series of gunshots in rapid succession cut through the thick ground fog in Owen Conagher's brain. He struggled out of unconsciousness into another kind of darkness, and for a moment did not know where he was.

He heard excited shouting from the street nearby, footsteps pounding along the boards, another exuberant yell.

As he tried to sit up, he realized that he lay in a soft bed, surrounded by strange perfumes. Fighting off dizziness and nausea, he struggled erect and swung his long legs to the floor. Knowledge of stepping through a window and seeing a door open returned in a rush as he looked up, and then it was all back.

He blinked slowly in surprise. They were still looking for him, even if what he heard from the street sounded more like a Fourth of July celebration than a man hunt. That meant that the woman who had come through the door—

He heard the knob turn and slapped his side instinctively —and felt only a naked hip.

She stepped quickly into the room and closed the door behind her. Reading her haste and secret manner, Conagher relaxed slightly, though he remained puzzled. He saw her slip past him in the darkness and fumble with something beside the bed. A match flared, and an instant later a glow widened as the wick of a candle burned higher.

The woman turned to face him—a plump woman with a rich fall of auburn hair and worried brown eyes, a green dress too tight for her generous curves.

"Nobody knows you're here," she blurted out.

"Figgered as much. I'm obliged to you."

She shook off his thanks. They studied each other in silence. She seemed to be trying to decide whether or not she should be frightened, and Conagher managed a faint smile.

"What's your name?" he asked.

"Lu-Anne."

"Lu-Anne. Uh-huh. That's right pretty."

She shrugged, pink shoulders lifting in the light of the Betsy candle beside the bed. "My ma give it me. I never liked it much. I don't know why men do."

"Maybe because it suits you."

Her brown eyes were skeptical. Conagher had a hunch the skepticism was frequently there, and with good reason.

"You haven't said who you were."

"Name's Conagher."

"That isn't what they call you. You're the killer they're lookin' for." It was not a question.

Conagher shook his head. "They're huntin' me, right enough, but I'm not what they think, nor who they think." He regarded her thoughtfully. "If you thought that, why didn't you yell?"

Lu-Anne hesitated, then gave another shrug. "I don't rightly know. I could see you were hurting."

He glanced down at his leg and felt a sudden heat of embarrassment. She had apparently tried to cut away his pants to expose the ugly wound in his thigh. Giving that up as a bad job, she had somehow managed to drag his jeans off. She had also opened his shirt and cut holes in his long underwear at his waist and along his left leg. The dirty jeans were in a pile on the floor near the washstand. A blood-soaked towel on the marble top of the stand beside the washbasin told of her efforts to clean away most of the dirt and blood from his wounds. Cleansed, the crease just below his rib cage didn't look like much. His leg, however, was a sorry-looking mess.

He looked up at her, startled.

"I dug the bullet out," she admitted, her face pale at the memory. "I . . . I could see it."

"I'll be damned."

"It seemed best to take it out while . . . while you couldn't feel nothin'."

"It was."

"You've got to get out of that shirt," she said abruptly. "Look what you've done to my bed. What did you do, fall into a garbage dump?"

"Somethin' like that."

"Well, you certainly smell like it."

Conagher smiled. The smell seemed to bother her more than his surprising tumble through her window, the bloody bullet she had extracted from his leg, or the possibility that she was alone in her room with a ruthless killer for whom the whole town was searching.

"I'm obliged to you," he said again. "But I'll be gettin' out of your way if you can find me some clothes."

"I doubt you could make it back through that window."

For the first time Conagher saw that she had drawn the curtains over the window. Before she lit that candle, he thought, wondering anew why she had not given him away.

"I can't stay here."

"You can for a while. No one will come lookin' for you here." She moved closer to the bed, and Conagher was strongly aware of the perfumed scent of her penetrating the vile smells that still clung to him. "Give me that shirt."

He was embarrassed again when she had to help him struggle out of the filthy shirt. He believed that his rest must have benefited him, but he was still weak. Lu-Anne carried the shirt away with an expression of distaste and dropped it onto the floor with the jeans. She added the bloody towel to the pile and removed another towel which had been soaking in the basin. She glanced at him as she wrung water from the towel, and Conagher flushed. In the remains of his underwear he felt as if he might as well have been stark naked.

Lu-Anne read his thought. "Don't be silly. I'm used to men. Don't you think I know what one looks like?"

"I suppose," he mumbled.

"You'll have to take that off, too. I can't have you smellin' up my room this way. Even if I could stand it, which I can't, anyone else would know you'd been here. That wouldn't do me any good. You can see that, can't you?"

Conagher refrained from pointing out that no one else knew he had fallen into a garbage pit.

"Can you find me some clothes?"

Lu-Anne smiled. "I reckon. There's more'n one man left this place in too much of a hurry to remember his pants. And I can dig up a shirt somewheres." She hesitated. "If I do that, will you take off that dirty underwear? And you can you wash up a little by yourself?"

Conagher nodded, relieved.

"All right. Don't be too long about it."

"I'd appreciate it if you was to hurry up with them clothes."

The woman sniffed derisively, but there was genuine amusement lurking at the corners of her mouth and in her eyes. She was a handsome woman, Conagher thought, with beautiful hair and a fine, ripe figure. The full bosom threatened to spill over the top of her bodice whenever she moved or bent over. The poor light in the room from the single candle was kind, however, to cruel traces of age and the ravaging effects of a hard life visible in the crow's feet around her eyes and the deepening lines framing her mouth. She was neither young nor innocent, but she had helped him simply because he was hurt, Conagher thought, and for no other good reason. Very possibly at some hazard to herself. Such women were often genuinely fond of men, he knew, and impulsively generous. The ironic contrast between her actions and the treatment he had received from the town's respectable citizenry could hardly escape him.

Lu-Anne slipped from the room, quickly closing the door. Painfully Conagher peeled off his underwear, which looked as if it had been attacked by giant moths. He threw it onto the floor with the rest of his clothes.

Naked except for his socks, Conagher grinned suddenly. Funny how a man could get fidgety in the presence of a strange woman—especially a handsome one.

He examined his wounds more closely. Lu-Anne had done a fair job of cleaning him up, but the hole in his thigh needed more than soap and water if he was to avoid having the flesh fester on him. He thought about the shallow penetration of the bullet, enabling Lu-Anne to see it. Not a direct hit, he thought, since no bone had stopped it. Must have been a ricochet.

He became conscious of the minutes dragging by. How long had she been gone? How could he be sure that she was looking for some pants and a shirt to fit him? Couldn't she have slipped down the stairs to warn someone of his presence—Selvy, even?

Frowning, Conagher shook off the suspicion. She had had plenty of time for that while he was unconscious and helpless. She deserved better of him.

He padded over to the washbasin and used the wet towel Lu-Anne had left there to wash away any lingering evidence of the garbage he had fallen into. He found a dry towel and was rubbing his body when Lu-Anne returned. Conagher hastily wrapped the towel around his loins, reddening when the woman laughed outright.

"You're no different from any other man."

"Never claimed I was," Conagher retorted with a shame-faced grin.

Along with the change of clothes, Lu-Anne had brought a half-empty bottle of whisky. "Mr. Parker don't allow no drinkin' upstairs," she explained. "There's been too much trouble over drinkin' in the rooms. But Sibyl—she's one of the girls—likes her own drink now and then. I got this from her."

"She know about me?"

"No."

Conagher nodded approvingly. He took the whisky and carried it over to the bed. Drawing the cork, he set his teeth and poured whisky directly over the raw wound in his leg. The room rocked as the pain hit him, and he was only dimly aware that Lu-Anne had run over to grab the bottle from him before it fell to the floor.

After that he sat woodenly on the edge of the bed while she tore another shirt—one of her own, he realized—into strips. Working silently and efficiently, she wrapped the fresh bandage tightly around his thigh and knotted the ends neatly.

"That'll have to do for a while," she said in a soft voice.

"It'll do just fine."

Smiling faintly, she watched him shrug into the shirt she had brought for him. It turned out to be a surprisingly good fit. Like the fresh jeans, it was worn but clean, having been washed since its last wearing. Conagher wondered idly about the owner or owners who had left in such a hurry. None had left his underwear behind, apparently, and Conagher didn't ask for any.

While he was working the tight jeans over his legs he asked about Parker.

"He's the man I work for. Owns the Dust Cutter—that's what this place is called. It ain't like him to allow what's been goin' on downstairs tonight."

"What's that?" Conagher asked, curious in spite of his eagerness to cover himself.

"Selvy has been buyin' drinks for every loafer in town,

seems like, gettin' them all likkered up before Deputy Reese swore them in. That ain't all. He's posted a reward for the one who finds you—five hundred dollars in gold!"

Conagher whistled softly. "Never figgered I was worth that much." He studied Lu-Anne thoughtfully, trying to assess what he had detected behind her words. "That money could've been yours."

She sniffed with exaggerated indifference. "Not that kind of money. And not from him."

"You don't much like Selvy, do you?"

Something in her eyes darkened. "Not much."

"You know him?"

"He's been up here," she said, stiffening unconsciously and compressing her lips. "A woman like me gets to see a man the way he really is. Seems like Mr. Selvy is laughing all the time, and that makes everyone like him . . . but he ain't always that way." She shivered, pink flesh quivering, and hugged herself with both arms as if she were cold. "I told Mr. Parker I'd quit before I'd have him up here again."

"I see."

There was defiance in Lu-Anne's eyes as they met his. "I may not be much, Conagher, but I know men. You don't have to tell me you're no hired killer. I could have said as much without you claimin' otherwise. And no one can tell me Selvy ain't mean and dirty inside, behind all the grinning."

Conagher stood to pull the borrowed jeans over his hips, mulling over what she had said, for some reason no longer self-conscious about having her watch him. The pants were a snug fit—he had had to grit his teeth while he tugged the left leg over his bandaged thigh—and he was sweating when he'd finished. He had to suck in his belly before he could stuff the shirt inside the waistband and snap it shut, but he knew the jeans would shape themselves to him after a while. They would do. He felt a lot better simply for being in clean clothes.

And he felt grateful. He rummaged around in his mind for the right words to say as much, without causing Lu-Anne to scoff at him, but he couldn't find anything adequate.

Buckling on his gunbelt, Conagher asked, "Where might I find this Selvy now?"

Lu-Anne hesitated. "He's downstairs."

Conagher looked up quickly. "Here?"

"He's in Mr. Parker's office. I guess he and the Reception Committee—that's what they call themselves—figured he'd be safe there."

Conagher took a turn toward the door. She stepped quickly into his path. "You can't go down there. They've posted sentries—they'd kill you before you could get halfway down the stairs."

Conagher eyed her narrowly, and for the first time she saw something hard and dangerous in him that she hadn't recognized before. From the moment he had stepped through the window into her room and collapsed, she had been involved with the fact of his being wounded and weak from loss of blood, a harassed man on the run who had awakened a woman's sympathy. While she had stripped his bloodied and torn jeans from him and tried to cleanse the bullet holes she had found in his side and one leg, she had felt a stirring response to him. His body was lean and hard-muscled, his belly flat and firm as a board. In repose, his weathered, rough-hewn features were almost handsome. She had remembered the quiet, almost gentle way he had first spoken to her—that, more than anything else, had kept her from crying out in alarm.

Now she saw that, however badly he had been hurt, he was not a man to be trifled with. He would not go down easily.

She found herself wondering where he had come from and where he was going, and what lay behind the loneliness in him that her own frequent loneliness and regret enabled her to sense.

Conagher relaxed, accepting her warning, and Lu-Anne understood that the danger in him was controlled and purposeful. It could not threaten her, unlike the streak of brutality she had discovered in Bud Selvy or the drunken ugliness that had been fired up tonight among the roustabouts and drifters in the Dust Cutter.

"Maybe you could go down and talk to Selvy," Conagher suggested. "Get him to come up here so's he can learn I'm not the killer he's scairt of. That's all I want—"

"He wouldn't listen to me," Lu-Anne said quickly. "And he wouldn't take any chances, don't you see that? He'd turn that whole wolf pack loose. Even if you could get away, there are other girls here. Someone would surely be hurt."

Conagher pondered this. Idly he fumbled in the pocket of the fresh shirt for the makings of a cigarette, before he remembered that it wasn't his own. Frowning, he crossed to the window and peered out between the curtains. The night was darker. Heavier cloud cover—the black storm clouds he had seen piling up over the mountains earlier—obscured moon and stars. The breeze had quickened, and there was the cool, heavy smell of coming rain in the air. That darker sky would make it safer for him to move about. But the street was even busier than before, noisier. He thought about Selvy buying drinks for any man in sight packing a gun . . .

"Is there anyone this Selvy would listen to?" he asked. "Someone ought to be able to tell him that the real killer might show up here any time, whilst he's busy lookin' the wrong way."

Lu-Anne started to shake her head, then caught herself. "There is someone—the only one I can think of. She works for him over at the freight line her pa used to run. I guess Selvy's stuck on her. That's what they say."

"Who might that be?"

"Willa Colgrove. You'd find her at her house—"

"I know," Conagher said, startling her. He examined the fact that he was not surprised. He remembered the tall girl with the strange violet eyes who had stepped through her doorway with a rifle aimed at his chest. The image was vividly clear, for he had thought of her several times at odd moments during the time since he had taken her Winchester and fled. He found himself smiling thinly at the memory. "So Selvy would listen to her?"

"How did you know? You couldn't—"

"We met," Conagher said briefly. "Not long enough to socialize. She tried to put a bullet in me."

"Oh."

"I reckon the problem might be to get her to listen to me. But if I could manage that, you think Selvy would hear her out?"

Lu-Anne was conscious of a sharp, irrational tug of feeling that was both strange and inexplicable, a quick response to the way Conagher had spoken of Willa Colgrove. She flushed, annoyed with herself and the idea that she could feel jealousy over this lean stranger.

"I'm sure he would. They say he's asked her to marry him."

"Uh-huh. That might explain a few things. Do they say the same about her?"

"I don't know," Lu-Anne answered shortly. She recalled meeting Willa Colgrove not long ago on the boardwalk. The girl had sensed Lu-Anne's appraisal and their eyes had met. She had smiled then, murmuring good morning before she passed on. The casual greeting had brought Lu-Anne a flush of pleasure. Perhaps it had meant little to the slim young woman, but she was the only respectable woman in Bitter Creek who had spoken to Lu-Anne during the year she had worked at the Dust Cutter. That memory prompted her to add, "I don't think he's sure of her. I think she keeps him guessing."

Conagher showed no reaction. After a moment he nodded, as if to himself. "It'll have to be her, then." She saw a new speculation shade his gray eyes. "But there's one other thing you can do for me."

"What's that?" She was surprised by her own eagerness.

"Tell me about this Reception Committee."

Lu-Anne was unable to identify all the men who had set up the ambush at the livery stables, but she named Ike Coolidge, the town banker; Isiah Howarth, a newspaperman; Reese, the deputy; and two others called Sanderson and Williams.

"Would one of them have a funny English accent?"

"That would be Mr. Williams. He has the pharmacy just up the street from the hotel."

"Who's Walsh?"

"Tug Walsh? He's a rancher in the valley—but I didn't know he was one of them."

Conagher was chewing over the information when there came a sharp knock on the door. Frightened, Lu-Anne stared at Conagher. There was no time for him to escape through the window. As the doorknob turned, he stepped quickly to the right of the door, easing behind it as it opened.

"Who is it—oh, Mr. Parker!"

"Where the hell you been, Lu-Anne?"

"I . . . I been sleepin' a little, that's all. I was tired."

"Damn it, you're not paid to sleep this time of night. Get downstairs."

"Yes, sir. I'll be right along."

She had placed herself to block the doorway, and her long skirts concealed the tumbled pile of dirty clothes and towels on the floor beside the washbasin.

"Smells like a garbage pail," the man in the hall commented. "You sure you're all right?"

"Well, I . . . I been a little sick. But I'm fine now."

"Well, why didn't you say so. If you're sick . . ."

"Really, I'm better now. I'll be down as soon as I clean up a little. It wouldn't do to leave this room smellin' like a garbage pail."

"Yeah. Well, whyn't you stay put for tonight," Parker said, mollified. "It ain't exactly a night for a woman who's been feelin' poorly."

As she closed the door on the sound of Parker's boots fading along the hall and starting down some nearby stairs, Conagher saw her smile, relieved and a little triumphant. Her eyes asked for his approval.

"Thanks," he said. "Your Mr. Parker don't sound like a bad sort to work for."

"Most of the time he's fair."

She was still standing with her back against the door when Conagher turned from the window to smile at her. "One other thing. Don't never let anyone tell you you're not much. Not even yourself."

He peered out, stepped through the window and was gone. For a long time she stared after him, not moving, while the curtains stirred gently in the freshening breeze.

TEN

The clamor of the fire bell awakened Willa Colgrove.

The evening had been a long one for her, filled with anxiety over the threat to Bud Selvy's life—a worry complicated by the unanswered questions in her mind concerning the tall stranger who had appeared on her porch. As the night wore on without news, she knew only that the hunt for the gunman continued, and that it was becoming something she liked less and less.

For a long time her father had sat out on the porch. Finally he went to bed, worn out, she knew, more by the pain he lived with constantly than by the long day and the late hour. She knew that he had disapproved of her threat to shoot the fugitive, although he had said little once the incident was over. For some reason he persisted in believing the stranger's claim of innocence.

At last, close to midnight, she lay on her bed in the darkness of her small room, knowing that she would not sleep with so much on her mind. She tried to concentrate on Selvy, going over exactly what he had said that evening, but her thoughts kept returning, unwillingly, to the moment the gunman had wrested the Winchester from her grasp. *I didn't think you'd do it.*

What had he meant? That he didn't believe she would try to shoot him? Or that he knew she would hesitate and fail in the attempt?

And what did it matter what he said or thought? He was a gunfighter, a hired killer, and she could think of nothing lower on this earth. Why should she remember so vividly the lean hardness of his body as he pinned her against the door, the way she had to look up to him, the strangely gentle tone of his voice?

Maybe he was not a killer.

But if that were true—if there was any chance at all that it was, as her father believed—then the wrong man was being hounded through the town by a growing pack of rowdies, shooting at the moon and baying like wolves. She shrank from the horror of this possibility.

Her thoughts turned restlessly away from the unthinkable. She had gone to her bed still wearing her long skirt and shirtwaist, believing that she would not sleep, that eventually a message would come from Selvy and she would have to be ready for it. She thought of getting up, for her clothes were surely becoming wrinkled beyond the possibility of another wearing, but she didn't. She lay waiting, wondering, and without realizing it, she slept.

The wild ringing of the bell brought a feeling of terror. What did it mean? That the hunt was over? No—that was the fire bell! It wouldn't be rung for anything else.

She struggled up. She had no idea how late it was or how long she had slept. The night was very dark. She ran for the west window. Instantly her gaze was riveted on the orange flames licking into the night sky. They came from somewhere at the west end of town, close to the business district, perhaps even one of the buildings on the main street.

Her fear leaped with the flames. The clamor of the bell went on insistently, and through its din came scattered shouts. The whole town would be awake now, frightened, for the danger of fire was everyone's danger. At this time of summer, dry for more than a month, the wooden buildings would burn like kindling if the fire reached them. Sparks would fly, and the hungry flames would jump from building to building, threatening the entire town . . .

She fumbled in darkness for her shoes, jerked them on, stumbled through the house to the front door. Her father appeared behind her in his nightshirt, limping painfully. He came to the door as Willa ran onto the porch and stopped to stare toward the smoke and flames that seemed to have climbed higher in the few seconds it had taken her to come from bedroom to porch.

She ran down the steps.

"Willa, come back here. You can't—"

"Pa, I must!"

"No, come back!"

But she ran on, heedless of his protest. A bucket brigade would be forming. Every able-bodied person had to help. The fire had to be contained quickly, if it was not already too late . . .

Willa raced through the night to the main street. There were other figures hurrying toward the street from all directions, men without shirts or hopping on one boot while they carried the other, women in hastily donned dresses, even a few children alerted by the general excitement and old enough to slip out of empty houses in defiance of dire warnings to stay put. The people began to come together as they hurried toward the fire barrel. A water wagon was already there, and it trundled off noisily as Willa arrived on the scene.

She could see the fire quite clearly then. It was at the west end of the street, behind the main row of false-fronted buildings. There were men on the nearby rooftops, starkly silhouetted by the orange glow of the fire.

Blurred questions flew around her. Shouts were thrown out and answered by other cries. A bucket brigade was already in action. Without hesitation Willa found a place in the line. Wordlessly room was made for her, another link in Bitter Creek's lifeline. In minutes she was lost in the frantic rhythm of the line, reaching out to receive a bucket that sloshed over with water, swinging the heavy bucket on to the next outstretched hands, turning to receive the next bucket, passing it on . . .

Her arms grew heavy. Sweat poured down her face and

bathed her body. She lost count of the number of buckets she had lifted and swung. For a time each effort brought agonizing pain. Then the pain dulled into an endless ache in her arms and across her back and shoulders, an ache that became one with the night, with the blurred faces and dim voices and the rumbling of the water wagon up and down the street and the flames that ate hungrily at the black curtain on the edges of her vision . . .

A half hour after Willa Colgrove's arrival, the worst danger was over. Exhausted, sweating and dirty from dust and smoke, Willa pieced together the story of the fire from fragments of news passed around among the fire fighters.

In the excitement she had completely forgotten about the grim search for the wounded gunman, and she had made no connection between that search and the fire. But one had led directly to the other. A few overeager members of the posse had thought the killer cornered in one of the storage sheds behind Dick Sanderson's feed and grain store. Stupidly—they had been drunk, one man said angrily—someone had decided to burn the man out of his hiding place. A fire had been started, and it had quickly engulfed the shed.

The gunman? No, she was told, he hadn't been there. But the fire had jumped to another shed, and showers of sparks soon threatened both the feed store and the adjoining buildings along the main street. The luck of a slackening in the wind—sign of a coming storm, someone said—had done more than the frantic efforts of the water brigade to contain the fire. Only Sanderson's sheds and part of his store had burned.

One man had been hurt in the fire, breaking a leg in a fall from one of the buildings adjacent to Sanderson's store. And there were unconfirmed rumors about Sanderson himself. He had run into the burning store. Someone said he had been dragged out alive, but others insisted that his fate was unknown.

Wearily Willa Colgrove turned back toward her house. Her arms and legs and shoulders ached beyond anything she could remember. There had been times during the past half hour when she didn't think she could lift another bucket. But she had, another and another after it. Now the weight of fatigue and strain descended upon her all at once.

She dragged herself along, stumbling, to the central intersection and turned right along the narrow side street. Her mind was numb. She wanted to see Bud Selvy, to reassure herself that he was all right, for she had not seen him among the fire fighters. He could hardly risk coming into the open, she realized, even in such a crisis. She wanted to know if the gunman had escaped, if he had caught a horse and fled, as someone in the street had claimed. She wanted to wait until the last smoking embers of the fire had been put out, but she knew she couldn't. She was no longer needed, and if she didn't get to her bed, she would find some place to curl up and go to sleep on the spot.

Exhausted, she was deaf and blind to her surroundings, unaware of movement behind her until the tall man was beside her. As she stiffened to cry out, he caught her arm and placed a hand firmly over her mouth.

Willa tried to push away. The man held her easily. He did not relax his grip or remove his hand from her mouth until she had stopped struggling.

"Will you hear me out before you yell?"

At Willa's hesitation he showed a flash of white teeth. She wondered how a hunted man could find it in him to smile.

"You got a way of rousin' the neighbors," Conagher said. "I got to be sure."

She jerked her head in angry agreement. Immediately he released her. Even then she thought of shouting, for surely she owed such a man nothing. But he seemed to sense this, waiting patiently for her reaction. Instead of yelling, she drew herself up—a gesture that had intimidated many men by itself—and glared at him. The pose had little effect, for he still looked down at her.

"I'm obliged," he drawled, as if he were amused with her. Before she could find a retort his tone sobered. "I'll be more obliged if you'll do somethin' for me."

"Why should I?"

His reply was without rancor. "Maybe because it's right to give any man a fair chance to be heard."

For some reason, the soft statement stung more than it should have. "All right, I'll listen," she answered stiffly. "But I'll promise you nothing. Don't expect me to—"

She broke off as someone trudged along the side street toward them. Conagher took her arm and steered her smoothly along the path toward her house. Willa flinched at his touch, but she did not resist or call for help. She had given her word, she thought. But did that explain it?

"I'll walk with you, if you don't mind," he murmured.

They walked in silence until the fall of other footsteps had faded into the darkness. Willa noticed that he still favored his left leg, and she sensed a deep fatigue in him that matched her own weariness of a few moments before—a feeling now astonishingly banished. Even in the dark she could see that his lean face was drawn, his mouth in repose a tight line. He was not an ugly or mean-looking man, she thought. His touch, like his voice, was gentle when that served, although there had been steel in his fingers when he held her while she struggled.

In that moment's silence she had time to calm her nerves and to sort out some of her thoughts. She was remembering some of the fragments of talk she had heard during the fire fight. Such as word that Harvey Parker had been buying drinks for all the loafers in the Dust Cutter before Deputy Reese swore them in as members of the posse. And news that Bud Selvy had offered a reward in gold to the man who brought the hunted killer down. Small wonder the town had almost burned, she thought. Surely it had been unnecessary to loose a drunken mob against the man who walked beside her.

But he was a killer. A man who made his living with his gun. There could be no rules in dealing with such a man. No one talked of fair play in hunting a marauding wolf . . .

Then why hadn't she cried out?

And why, walking beside him, drawing close to the front porch of her home, was she not frightened?

"I know what you think," Conagher said. "That I'm supposed to be a gunman lookin' for this man Selvy. And I have no reason to expect you to believe me when I tell you you're wrong, just like the rest of this friendly town. But it's a fact, all the same. They jumped the wrong man, is all. I don't know why they picked on me. Maybe because they were expectin' someone to come along when I did, or maybe because I look like what this bad man is supposed to. Anyways, I figger there might still be a chance to straighten it out before this whole town goes up in smoke. You could help."

Startled, Willa Colgrove halted beside the low fence that fronted her yard. She wondered if her father was watching from the front window. Crippled as he was, he could still handle a gun, and he would if he thought her threatened.

But this man before her had no intention of harming her.

Did he mean harm to anyone?

For the first time, Willa squarely and openly faced the possibility that the stranger might be telling the truth— that he was not the gunman Selvy feared. A tremor of shock ran through her. She realized that she had been rejecting this very possibility for hours, refusing to accept it, and the acknowledgment was a painful one.

"Why me? Even if I would agree, why did you pick me?"

"Because I reckon this Selvy ought to know the man who's chasin' him. And you can talk to Selvy better than anyone else."

She stared at him in amazement. "How do you know that?"

"Another woman told me." He seemed to smile faintly. He wasn't a man who smiled a lot, she thought, unlike Bud Selvy. But there was a strong strain of humor in him that refused to be quashed even when he was hunted and in pain.

Was that the description of a killer? Or did such men fit into any mold? Might not a gunfighter have a quiet voice and easy smile? What did she know of such things at all?

"Well, I don't know what she told you . . ."

"She said Selvy was sweet on you."

Willa Colgrove blushed. She didn't know what to say. She certainly was not going to discuss her private life with a complete stranger, especially this battered man on the run whose word she had no reason to trust, aside from some irrational impulse she did not understand. But why did it make her uncomfortable to have him think there was some special relationship between her and Selvy? It was true, after all. He had asked her to marry him, and if she had not accepted him, she had not refused him outright, as she had turned down other men in the past. She had accepted the possibility—and tonight she had finally told her father that she would marry him.

Willa tried to be detached, objective. She would hear this man out. Then she would decide what she would do. What he had heard or what he thought was unimportant.

"What is it you want me to do? I don't really see how I can help you."

"I want to get a message to Selvy, that's all. And you could take it. He'd listen to you. That's all I want."

"What kind of a message?"

"I want to see him, is all. And I want him to see me. If he knows this gunman he's so scairt of, then he'll know I'm not that man."

Willa felt a quick resentment of the casual reference to Selvy's fear, an impulse to defend him, but she swallowed her retort. After all, he *was* afraid. That was what the Reception Committee was all about, wasn't it? And wasn't that why an unruly pack of drunken hooligans threatened to destroy the town before this night was over?

She had tried to justify Selvy's actions, but from the beginning she had been uneasy over his willingness to accept the role of the committee in protecting him. She found herself wondering now what the tall stranger beside her would have done if he had been in Selvy's boots. And without any sound basis for the judgment, she was certain that he would have handled his own fight, whatever it was.

He sought her help now, but for a different reason. Not to run from a fight, but to face his accuser.

Willa felt guilty over the comparison. It was disloyal to the man who had helped her father through his crisis, who had kept her on at the freight line when it might have been easier to let her go and to sever all connection between the line and its former owners, who had, finally, courted her and offered her marriage. But in spite of her inclination to wriggle away from it, the contrast between Selvy's actions and those of the stranger were unpleasantly clear—and Selvy came out smaller in every way.

"Do you want me to take you to him?"

"Doubt that'd be wise. The way things are in town, there's too many might want to take a shot at that reward, and I wouldn't want to put you in the way of that."

The reward. Yes, that was the most disturbing news of all. It had made the hunt for this man an uglier blood sport. And what he said was true. The same drunken rowdies who had recklessly fired Sanderson's shed could not be trusted to hold their fire if the gunman walked boldly among them, even if she were at his side and he carried a white flag.

But something about the stranger's request had been disturbing her, and suddenly she saw what it was. Suspicion leaped into her eyes. "Then you want me to arrange a meeting, is that it?"

"That's right."

"Some place private? Where he would come alone?"

"Uh-huh." The tall man caught the sharpness of her tone and gazed at her speculatively.

"So's you can gun him down," Willa said scornfully.

Conagher was silent a moment. "I can see how you might look at it that way. It's not what I had in mind."

"How can I be sure of that?"

He shook his head, a wry smile forming. "Reckon you can't. I can only give you my word on it."

"The word of a killer!"

Conagher's gaze was steady and unflinching as it met hers. They were good eyes, she thought unexpectedly. Thoughtful and quiet, they had regarded her, she was certain, with humor but also sometimes with admiration. She found no guile in them now. Was he clever enough to hide that from her?

"Do you really believe that?"

She surprised herself. "No."

Conagher nodded, as if something important had been settled between them. "Then you don't have to worry. I have no cause to gun Selvy down, savin' what he's given me this night. Maybe he can explain that mistake. I'm willin' to talk that out if you can think of a place we could get together."

Willa Colgrove wondered at the ease with which she made her decision. The only explanation she could give was that, unaccountably, she trusted this tall, soft-spoken man. She even *liked* him, which was the most astonishing thing of all. She was aware of growing curiosity and ungrudging respect for the kind of man who could so calmly accept the possibility of a "mistake" that had almost cost him his life —and might still claim it.

Unless she was willing to help.

She heard herself say, "All right. I'll try."

"Good. You know this town. Maybe you can pick out a

place I could wait, where Selvy can come without anyone wonderin' too much what he's up to."

The answer came quickly. Not Selvy's Mercantile, which was on the main street and surrounded by potential trouble for the stranger. The freight-line office, on the other hand, was on the north side of town toward the west end, away from the main street. Selvy could go there without raising any questions. Moreover, the gunman—she had to find another way of identifying him—ought to be able to reach the yard unseen by circling east and north of the town. All he needed was a key to the office, where he could wait safely—and she could provide that.

She explained her choice. "Mr. Selvy owns the freight line. No one will question him going there if he chooses."

The tall man nodded approvingly. "I'll wait for him there."

Willa took her office key from her pocket. She hesitated only briefly before handing it to him. "I don't know who you are," she said slowly. "If you're not the one they call Rorke . . ."

He smiled. His eyes looked deep into hers, and for some reason she felt her heart skip. "Name's Conagher, Miss Colgrove. And you can tell your pa—he's waitin' for you there on the porch—that he can put that shotgun away. I've no intentions of carryin' you off, even though the notion is mightily tempting."

And with that he accepted her key and moved off, visibly limping.

Turning, Willa caught the dull gleam of her father's shotgun where the barrel projected beyond the cover of the porch roof. Little of it showed, but the man called Conagher had known all along that Dan Colgrove was there.

When Willa swung back to peer after Conagher, he had disappeared.

ELEVEN

A wicked light gleamed in Bud Selvy's eyes. "He's there now? In the freight office?"

"I expect so. I gave him my key so he could let himself in. I told him you'd come alone."

"That was smart, Willa. Real smart." Selvy's grin matched the cunning glint in his eyes, and for the first time since she had found him in Harvey Parker's office at the Dust Cutter, she felt a stab of concern.

"Did I do the right thing?"

"You did fine—you did perfect." Selvy, who had been sitting behind Parker's handsome mahogany desk when she was ushered into the office—it was the first time she had ever set foot inside the saloon—came around it now to place his hands on her shoulders. She was aware of their eyes meeting at the same level, where she had had to look up to meet Conagher's gaze. "I couldn't have asked for better. Now you go on home and stay there until this is over."

"You'll go to meet Conagher?"

Selvy's grin curled into something nasty. "His name's Rorke, no matter what he told you. He'll get the meetin' he wants, only not the way he's tried to get it up."

"Bud! Don't you believe me?"

"I believe everythin' you say, honey. But that slick killer don't fool me for a minute." Releasing her, he turned to the sallow-faced Parker, who had personally escorted her past the grinning men in the saloon with an odd show of courtly manners. "Get aholt of Reese and Hanson and bring 'em in here. And Tug Walsh, if you can find him."

"What about the rest of the committee?"

"Forget them." There was the sharpness of a command in Selvy's words, and Parker left immediately.

"No, Bud—wait. You can't! I believe what Conagher told me. He's not the man you think."

Selvy chuckled. The short laugh held condescension. "So he took you in, huh? I wouldn't of thought any man could make a fool of you, Willa."

"But he didn't. I'm sure of it!"

"Sure enough to let me risk a bullet?" A coldness subtly altered Selvy's ever-present smile. "It's too bad I won't be able to hear him give his spiel. I'd kinda like to hear it. I'd like to hear the man who could turn your head this way."

"But I gave my word he'd be safe there! I said you'd come alone."

"He fooled you, Willa. Face up to it. Your word don't matter when he was only usin' you to get at me. You'll see that when you calm down enough to think it out."

Parker returned, followed by the heavy-shouldered deputy who worked at the hotel. She had always despised Reese for the way his eyes moved hungrily over her body whenever he saw her, even when she was just passing through the lobby, as if, knowing that he could never have her, he took a perverse pleasure in insolent appraisal. A red-faced man whom she didn't recognize, addressed by Selvy as Hanson, accompanied Reese. With mounting consternation Willa heard Selvy give terse orders to round up the posse and to surround the freight yard and office buildings.

"You sure he's there?" Reese asked. His speech was slurred, and Willa realized that he had been drinking heavily. His gaze moved slowly over her, and she felt herself reddening.

"Sure enough," Selvy said sharply. "Now get a move on!"

"No!" Willa cried. "I won't let you do this. I told you I gave him my word—"

Selvy's swift reaction silenced her. "You'd try to warn him, wouldn't you?"

"Yes!"

Willa stared at him. She saw a man she didn't know, the secret man behind the ready grin, someone ruthless and implacable, whose cruel gaze cut into her with the chill of a winter wind searching out a weakness.

That cold gaze judged her now with something like contempt.

"Then you'll stay here," Selvy said.

"You can't make me . . ."

Ignoring her, Selvy turned toward the door. He pushed the others ahead of him, Harvey Parker among them. Blocking the doorway with his broad bulk, he stared back at her. "There's no window, so it's no good lookin' for a way out. I'll post a man outside this door, so you won't be disturbed. No one will bother you. If anyone tries it, he'll answer to me."

"To you?" Scorn filled her voice with loathing. "Or to some other committee who'll do it for you?"

Bud Selvy flushed an angry red. For a long moment he studied her, no longer smiling, no longer tolerant and amused. "I'll put that down to you bein' upset, and not bein' in your senses. I don't know what that hardcase killer did to poison your mind, but it gives me one more reason to make sure he's put under. You'll apologize when this is over—"

"Never!"

Selvy's smile reappeared, but there was nothing pleasant about it. It was no more than an habitual twist of his lips. In the heat of outrage she wondered what she had ever found attractive in him, how she had ever come to believe him a man of worth and humor.

"You will. Better get used to the idea. Just like you better get used to the idea of marryin' me."

"Never! I'll die first."

"You may think you want to die, but you don't. No one does. And I'm gonna have you, one way or another—whatever way you want it. I've waited long enough."

The angry slam of the door punctuated his promise. Willa started toward it. She stopped abruptly as she heard the lock click.

She was locked in.

Trapped. As surely as the man called Conagher was trapped.

And she had led him into it, believing that she could trust him, never dreaming that she could not trust the man she had intended to marry.

Owen Conagher had unlocked the door to the freight office with Willa Colgrove's key. After a quick survey of the outer room, another that was obviously used by the owner as his private office, and a small storage room, he went back outside. The wind was rising again, carrying its scent of rain. Now and again lightning danced among the distant peaks to the west, and there was a low rumble of thunder. Conagher wondered if the storm would come in time to dampen the enthusiasm of the vigilantes.

It wouldn't matter if Selvy agreed to come.

Moving as quickly as he could with his dragging leg, Conagher searched the wagon yard and inspected the corral, where a dozen horses and half as many mules were stirring about restlessly, scenting the approaching storm. He checked the relationship of several small outbuildings to the office. When he was satisfied that the place was empty of any immediate threat, he gazed thoughtfully at the dark mass of buildings along the main street to the south and the few scattered houses intervening.

He didn't like it.

The idea of this meeting had been his, and, liking the girl, he had held out a small hope that it might work. The kind of man who had courted her, a man she had approved enough to accept his courtship, might be enough like her to accept the face-to-face confrontation Conagher had suggested. He might be—but Conagher couldn't count on it. He had ridden into one ambush this night. He wouldn't place himself in another trap.

There would be time enough to show himself when Selvy appeared alone at the freight yard.

North of the yard, a line of brush and trees drew Conagher to the creek, which curled around the town on the north side. Beyond the creek rose a shallow bluff. Conagher waded across the stream and limped along the bank until he found a place where he could climb the bluff readily, not trusting his leg to manage any hard climbing. Moving hastily now, for he reckoned that he didn't have much time, he searched out a vantage point that allowed him to peer between the curly heads of two cottonwoods toward the freight yard. He had a good view of the office building and the wagon yard and a corner of the corral. He could not see the front of the main building.

Conagher lay flat on a rock ledge, protected by the shadow of a crease. He glanced toward the black sky. There was little likelihood of his being spotted, but the darkness obscured his own view.

He didn't have long to wait.

He heard them coming along the creek long before he saw anything. Several men crept along the edge of the stream, hugging the bank. Once Conagher heard the splash of a boot in the water, followed by a muttered curse. He waited, watching the black shine of the water through an opening in the brush. A solid shadow moved across the opening. Then another.

In the next five minutes he estimated that at least a dozen men fanned out behind the freight yard, although he could not see clearly enough to count. There would be as many more, he guessed, covering the front, forming a circle around the entire area.

At some unseen signal the dark shapes crept away from the creek bed and drew closer to the cluster of buildings and yards, pulling the noose tighter. A noose that would have closed around his neck if he had been in the office.

Anger lashed him.

Had the woman betrayed him? The idea came hard, and he didn't want to accept it. He had trusted her as he had asked her to trust him.

Or had Selvy simply refused to heed her? Had he listened to Conagher's message and refused to accept the possibility that it might be true?

That seemed more plausible. It allowed Conagher to retain an impression of Willa Colgrove that he was reluctant to lose. A man who stayed in hiding while others did his fighting for him, whatever the odds, was unlikely to be a trusting man. More likely he was a nervous one, quick to jump at any chance to eliminate a threat, too cautious to gamble on the word of a stranger or the possible gullibility of a woman.

His woman.

Conagher found that he didn't enjoy thinking of Willa Colgrove that way. He grinned wryly. Hell of a time to be entertaining foolish notions about any woman, or to be remembering the willowy strength and softness of this one. Hell of a time to think about anything but getting out of this scrape with his neck still short.

Someone yelled. Selvy? Conagher doubted it. He was filling in details of the man, and what he came up with aroused contempt. Selvy was still safe in his hole, probably still at the Dust Cutter as Lu-Anne had said.

"Rorke? You might as well come out. You ain't gonna skin out of this one."

Conagher couldn't see who was doing the calling. He was somewhere out front. And if he had any sense, he was behind some cover.

"We'll smoke you out, Rorke, one way or another. Might as well make it easy on yourself. Throw out your gun, and follow it with your hands high, and you'll get a fair shake."

Smiling thinly, Conagher wriggled away from the bluff's edge until he was beyond the sight line from the freight yard. He rose stiffly. Time to move along. If they decided to fire the office building, there would be too much light around here for him to escape notice. The whole town might become a giant torch if the vigilantes weren't careful . . .

He had covered some forty yards, working along the broken terrain north of the creek, when the night exploded in a thunderous volley of gunfire.

Conagher pulled up to listen. The shooting continued without letup for a full minute. Then it fell off into a more sporadic crackling of shots. He could hear the occasional slam of a shotgun and the crack of rifles mixed in among the lesser gunfire, and after a while each shot jarred him with an almost physical impact. Every one of those bullets was meant for him. Every chunk of lead was meant to cripple or kill . . . him. Every falling hammer was an act of violence . . . against him.

And every shot fed his rising anger.

He was clear of them now. When they had finally worked up enough pack courage to storm the freight office, or burn it to the ground, they would turn elsewhere. He could sneak back and steal one of those horses from the corral, and by first light he could be a long jump ahead of any pursuers, running ahead of the storm to let it wash out his tracks. And most of the vigilantes would be in no shape to last out a long chase.

He could . . . but he was through running.

None of this was his choosing. He had done his best to stop it, and Selvy's answer was another ambush.

Conagher was bone-tired. His eyes were grainy and raw, his side ached, his leg throbbed intolerably. His belly was growling from going empty. If the vigilantes were in poor shape, he was in worse.

He thought about the town, so pretty in the twilight when he had first glimpsed it far below him. It was a different place now, a town gone crazy. It was too late for anyone to listen to him. He had seen it happen before. He had seen other towns go crazy with fear or panic or a frenzied blood lust. Bitter Creek was like that now.

But he wasn't running any more.

There had been a Reception Committee, Lu-Anne had said. Selvy's committee. They were the leaders of the hunt. If he couldn't get at Selvy directly, he might reach some of the committee. He even knew most of their names.

Grimly, hearing another small volley of gunfire from the freight yard, Owen Conagher turned toward the creek and, beyond it, the restless town that was forcing him into a fight he had not wanted.

TWELVE

Rafe Quinn stared at the locked door of Harvey Parker's office, thinking of the woman inside. She was a woman to think about. He had thought so before, just about every time he had seen her around town or at the freight-line office.

The notion of unlocking that door, which he was supposed to be guarding, teased him. Parker and Selvy had stepped outside when all the shooting was heard from the north side of town, but they might return at any moment. And Sam Cowens, the bartender, could see Quinn and the office door.

Scowling, Quinn tried to push the reckless idea away.

Hell, he needed another drink. There was no need for him to stand outside the door. It was too heavy, too solid for any woman to break out. She wasn't going anywhere.

He had a drink at the bar. Cowens, who had a way of not seeing what he didn't want to see, turned his back and polished some glasses. Quinn leaned an elbow on the thick, curving edge of mahogany and surveyed the barroom. It was almost empty. Nearly everyone was with the posse or out on the boardwalk listening to the fireworks. One of Harvey Parker's dealers was flipping cards onto a table, cheating himself. None of Parker's girls was around. He had sent them all to their rooms alone. That plump one Quinn hankered after, Lu-Anne, hadn't been around all night. . .

Quinn's gaze roved up the stairs to the balcony. Hadn't seen her downstairs at all, but she had been in her room, for he had seen Parker at her door once, talking to her. He could see the door now. It was closed, like the others. It was late, and . . .

An idea flickered in his brain, like a light glimpsed over a far distance.

He glared suspiciously at Cowens. The bartender still had his back to Quinn. No one in the nearly empty saloon was paying attention to him. There was still the sound of gunfire over by the freight yard where the gunman had been cornered, and that was keeping the curious out on the boardwalk.

Rafe Quinn glanced upstairs, thinking of Lu-Anne. He felt a thick stirring in his blood.

At that moment the dealer playing solitaire at one of the tables rose and walked past Quinn to the front of the saloon. He paused a moment before the swinging doors, then stepped outside.

Without a conscious moment of decision, Rafe Quinn started toward the stairs. He had been drinking heavily all night—he wasn't one to hang back when someone was buying free whisky—and he stumbled on the first step. He looked up to find Cowens's eyes on him. Quinn glared the bartender down. When Cowens turned away, Quinn resumed climbing the stairs, stepping carefully as a drunken man will, making exaggerated efforts to keep his balance.

From the balcony he looked down. The saloon was empty. Cowens was carefully tending to his business behind the bar.

A sly grin appeared on Quinn's face, which had a puffed and reddened appearance from drinking, the vice which had twice nearly cost him his job as a drover with Selvy's freight line. He moved along the uncarpeted balcony, going up on his toes to make as little noise as possible.

He put his ear to Lu-Anne's door. Nothing. That meant little, for she might be asleep in that soft bed of hers. She'd be glad of a little company.

There were no locks on any of the doors to these small rooms off the balcony. Harvey Parker didn't place much importance on privacy for his girls, and there were occasions when he wanted quick access to the rooms in the event of trouble. Rafe Quinn gave one last glance at the empty saloon below and stepped quickly into the room.

It was dark. Quinn left the door open a crack to admit a faint light. He heard the woman stir sleepily in the bed, sheets rustling, and his heart began to pound as heat surged to his loins.

He saw a small lamp on a bedside table. Striking a match, Quinn closed the door behind him.

Lu-Anne was sitting up when Quinn touched his match to the candle and the small room brightened. "Who is it?" Her eyes, puffy with sleep, widened. Quinn stared at her bare shoulders and arms as she hugged her blankets over her bosom.

She was fully awake now. "Get out," she said sharply. "I'm not seein' anyone tonight. I been . . . sick."

"You don't look sick to me," Quinn said with a grin.

Then he smelled it. Puzzled, he turned to survey the room. The smell was strong, like old garbage, and there was the sharp, sweet smell of blood mixed with it. Maybe she had been sick. Hell, it was just his luck to get her alone like this and find her sick.

He discovered the stained and bloody shirt hidden in a corner of the room. He picked it up. It was a man's shirt. The blood was recent.

Lu-Anne was staring at him in fright. As Rafe Quinn's whisky-dulled brain slowly worked over the meaning of a bloody shirt in her room on this particular night, she slid from the bed on the side away from him. Her glance darted toward the door, but he was closer to it. She edged away from him toward the open window.

"What the hell's this? By God, it was him! You had him in here—that gunman!"

"No, I . . . I was sick, I told you. You'd best get out of here before Mr. Parker comes."

"He's outside," Quinn said angrily. He checked the momentary feeling of outrage. What did he care how the killer had come to her room or what had happened here? What was plain was that no one else knew—and that she didn't want anyone to know. There must have been other evidence of the wounded man's presence in her room, but she had removed it—foolishly keeping the shirt for whatever reason.

His sly grin reappeared as he took a step toward her. "Parker don't have to know. We can keep it between us two. Just you and me. Hell, I don't give a damn-all who you been keepin' company with, long as there's room for me."

He threw the bloodstained shirt aside carelessly. Lu-Anne retreated toward the window. Her eyes darted this way and that, like those of a frightened animal. Quinn crowded her, his gaze on the pink softness of her shoulders and the swelling bosom she tried ineffectually to cover with her arms. Lust raked his body, goading him like spurs.

"Ain't no need to get flighty with me," Quinn said.

"Get away from me!" She spat the words at him.

Angered, Rafe Quinn lunged for her. She twisted away from him as his hand closed on her thigh. Before he realized what she was up to, she was through the window. He grabbed at her leg and ripped the trailing skirt of her nightgown.

For a moment they struggled, the woman halfway out the window. Quinn felt her slipping away from him and he swore aloud. Lu-Anne cried out.

He tumbled through the window after her onto the outside balcony. She almost eluded him, but Quinn held onto a piece of her gown. He felt the soft fabric tear, and she was free.

Spinning away from him, Lu-Anne tripped and fell.

That gave Quinn the time he needed to catch her as she jumped to her feet. Her momentum carried them along the balcony toward the front of the building.

Rafe Quinn caught her at the corner. Driven by lust and drunken rage, he had forgotten Parker, Selvy, the hunted gunman, everything but this pink-fleshed woman who was his to take. He heard her screams only dimly, as if the sound had nothing to do with her or with him. Her fingers raked at his eyes and he hit her solidly.

He felt her sag from the blow, but when his arms pulled her toward him, trying to drag her away from the front balcony overlooking the street, she thrashed violently, breaking his hold. Her knee drove painfully into his groin.

Breath exploded from his lungs as pain shot through him. He struck blindly, smashing his fist into her face.

Falling, she tumbled against the front railing. The top bar broke with a crack like a gunshot. Rafe Quinn heard her whimpering cry and reached for her, feeling a stab of alarm. He caught only another piece of fabric. The railing behind her gave way and she plummeted from sight.

Passion and anger drained out of Quinn as swiftly as Lu-Anne had plunged to the street. He stood near the broken rail, swaying. A hand pawed at his eyes as if he wanted to wipe away the image of her falling.

Behind him a voice spoke in cold anger. "You son of a bitch!"

Rafe Quinn turned. Harvey Parker, who had emerged from a side door onto the balcony, stood ten feet away.

"I didn't mean . . ."

The small gun in Parker's hand spat twice, stitching two neat holes hardly an inch apart in Rafe Quinn's chest. The impact of the small caliber bullets was not enough to knock him down. For a moment he stood there, still swaying, staring down in a daze at his chest. Clumsily he wiped at the button-size holes, surprised by the swift seepage of blood.

"Oh, hell," Quinn said.

His big body tipped over the broken railing and he dropped like a sack of wet grain to the ground below.

There was a moment of shocked silence when the second body tumbled from the balcony to land in the street near Lu-Anne's crumpled form. Several men ran from the boardwalk to surround the woman. Another, a cowpuncher named Davis, bent over Rafe Quinn. He saw instantly that the big man was dead.

Sobered, Davis felt a chill, as if a bitter wind had swept along the street. He looked up at the empty balcony.

Another rattle of gunfire from the direction of the freight yard caught his ear.

Violence had been loosed in Bitter Creek, and now the guns of darkness had brought death to its dusty main street.

And it was not over, the shaken cowhand thought as he rose. He glanced uneasily around, as if death were a specter on horseback he might see. He felt a sudden longing for open spaces and sober work.

Davis started along the street away from the Dust Cutter. Someone growled a question at him. "Dead," the cowboy muttered.

His steps quickened, and soon he broke into an unsteady trot, heading for the corral where his horse had been left. He could feel a pressure against his back like a hand pushing, and he knew it was the hand of fear.

He heard a shout but paid no heed. He had had enough. There was another shout, and he broke into a run. He was sweating now, and afraid.

Then a gun spoke, a thin sharp crack of sound, and the hand at his back struck him like a fist, driving him off his feet, spilling him onto his face in the dust.

Davis lifted his head once and choked out his protest. He was filled with a sense of the ridiculousness of this way of dying. Then the meaning of his protest slipped away from him, and there was only the awful darkness.

THIRTEEN

The man called Rorke left Colton quietly, without a word to anyone, early in the evening. The desk clerk at the hotel, Beddoes, saw him leave, for he was an alert man, and too many tried to depart without paying their bills. Rorke was not one of these, but if he had been, Beddoes wondered, would he have had the nerve to call him on it? The way Rorke stared at you with those cold eyes . . .

Jimmy Wooster, a sixteen-year-old hostler at the corral where Rorke had kept his chestnut gelding, brought the horse when Rorke called for it and watched the gunman saddle up. Recounting the details of the meeting would make Wooster a temporary hero among the youngsters of Colton. There was no question about which horse belonged to Rorke, but, as Jimmy said, he could have picked any old horse he wanted.

The cold-eyed gunfighter had been in Colton exactly seven days, and without ever pulling either of the twin Colts he wore, he had left his mark.

He had left it on a shaken Burt Angstrom, who had proffered the information Rorke sought about a man named Niles Asher, whose description remarkably matched that of Bud Selvy of Bitter Creek, a day's ride to the southeast across the Cove Mountains. When Rorke had finally come to Angstrom with his questions, Angstrom had tried to be evasive, out of a vague loyalty to Sanderson and Selvy—and a certain concern for business relationships. Rorke had stared at him steadily, his hooded gray eyes like pale agates. Angstrom had faltered, stumbled, finally pulled up lame. Rorke continued to stare at him without a word for the ticking of a full minute. By the end of it, Burt Angstrom could feel the hairs standing straight out at the back of his neck.

He had hastily stammered out the information Rorke wanted. The gunman had left without comment. That night, for the first time in many years, Angstrom had knelt beside his bed and prayed for his immortal soul. He had had a glimpse of how near death could be.

Rorke rode steadily through the evening. His ruddy-colored horse, which had a distinctive apron face, was fresh and strong and eager. They reached Ike Higgins's stage stop at Long Neck Pass before midnight. Rorke methodically saddled down, even for the short stopover he planned. He paid for a sparse meal and a bunk, and rolled into the latter almost immediately. He slept, Higgins noted, with his gun out of the leather. It was hidden under his blanket, but Higgins was convinced that the man slept with his gun in his hand. "Hell, I wouldn't be surprised if'n it was cocked!" he said·later.

The gunfighter slept for a little over two hours. He had ascertained the distance to Bitter Creek precisely, and he knew that he would reach the valley in the last hour of darkness, his approach unnoticed until the moment he chose to reveal himself.

The man he knew as Niles Asher, who now called himself Bud Selvy, would be expecting him.

He saddled up and rode away from the landing, as quietly as he had come, shortly after two in the morning. It had started to rain.

At about the same time the silent gunman rode away from Higgins's Summit Lodge, Alfred Williams sat up on his cot in the room behind his pharmacy. He listened intently, his heart pounding. Then he heard again the tapping on his back door which had awakened him from fitful sleep.

Stepping quickly to the small window at the back of the room, he tried to peer through a parting in the burlap curtain. It was pitch black outside and he could see nothing.

Nervously Williams went to the door. "Who is it?" he called out. "Who's there?"

"Selvy."

He shuddered in relief. The feeling was short-lived. What did Selvy want now? He had done his best—all he could. He wanted only to be left out of it now. What had begun as a noble civic enterprise, a chance to align himself with the leading citizens of Bitter Creek in an adventure that lived up to his high expectations in coming to the American West to make his mark, had turned into something else, a savage hunt for which he had quickly felt himself inept.

"What do you want, Mr. Selvy?"

Selvy said something inaudible. Suddenly it occurred to Alfred Williams that Selvy had emerged from his hiding place in the saloon. That could mean only one thing—the hunt was over. That was why he had come. The whole sorry affair was over.

Eagerly Williams drew the bolt and opened the door. "You caught the fellow? Is he dead? I don't mind saying—"

The door slammed inward, twisting his wrist painfully as a tall man stepped inside. "Not dead yet," the man said curtly.

He kicked the door shut and seized Williams by the neck of his shirt. He had lain on his cot fully dressed, having removed only his stiff collar. The tall man twisted the handful of shirt until the neck tightened painfully. Williams struggled futilely, shaking with terror.

"Name's Conagher," the man said softly. "And we got some talkin' to do."

"I . . . I don't know you! I say . . . please!"

"You tried to kill me. That's knowing enough."

"No, no . . . really. That's impossible. We were only—"

"You picked on the wrong man, is all. And now some-one has to ante up. You're the first."

"Oh, my God . . ."

Alfred Williams collapsed. In a helpless state he was picked up bodily and carried into his shop. There Con-agher set him in a chair and pushed him erect when he started to sag. The second time he nearly fell, Conagher slapped him, hard enough to bring tears to Williams's eyes. That pulled him out of his swoon, at least enough for him to sit up in his chair and stare at his nemesis with bulging eyes.

He saw a drawn, remarkably ordinary-looking man, quite unlike the brutal killer he had imagined. But there was a steely glint in Conagher's eyes that warned him of danger real and close. He was convinced that his life de-pended on what he said or did now. The man was near ex-haustion and in great pain, Williams saw . . . and he was angry.

"You're one of the Reception Committee."

"No, uh—"

"Don't lie to me."

"Well, I—"

"I ought to kill you now. I'm supposed to be a cold-hearted killer, ain't that right?"

Williams could only stare at Conagher mutely. There was no possible answer. Was it conceivable that they had all been wrong? That this was not the gunman pursuing Bud Selvy? The consternation awakened by this appalling possibility appeared in Williams's eyes, and the haggard man before him nodded.

"That's right. So can you think of a good reason why I shouldn't kill you?"

"It . . . it wasn't my idea. It was Ike Coolidge's—and Selvy's. It was really for Selvy—we did it for him!"

The tall man dragged up another small, cane-backed chair and sat astride it. "Suppose you tell me about it."

Alfred Williams did, eagerly setting forth the whole story as far as he knew it, commencing with Dick Sanderson's return from Colton with news of the gunmen and Selvy's determination to leave town. "Sounds right civic-minded," Conagher murmured at that point.

When the pharmacist had finished his tale, Conagher remained silent for a minute, as if he were weighing the truth of it, causing Williams to exclaim, "It's the truth, I swear it! That's the whole story!"

At length the tall man pushed out of his chair and, scowling, prowled along the aisle before the glass display case. Williams noted that he dragged his left leg, favoring it, and that there was a dark stain seeping through his tight jeans. Conagher paused, staring at the display case and the rows of bottles arrayed on the shelves behind it, as if he were seeing their contents for the first time.

His speculative gaze moved along to the Manton rifle which Williams had returned to its case, mounted on the wall over the door to his back room. Williams's heartbeat jumped as Conagher's hard glance accused him before it returned to the rifle.

"That what you used at the stables to shoot me with?"

"I'm sure it wasn't my bullet that struck you, sir," Williams protested. "I'm not a sportsman at all, really—"

"Sport? That what you call it?"

"Uh, no, I didn't mean . . ."

Conagher grunted. "This thing shoot as good as it looks?"

"It . . . it's dead accurate."

The tall man smiled thinly. "Depends on who's at the other end, don't it?"

Williams tried to return the smile, but he couldn't quite manage it. He was still not certain what Conagher intended to do to him, and when his thoughts drifted in-

evitably in that direction, he lurched away from the dread
possibilities.

"I'll take it along, if you don't mind."

"Not at all . . . please do!"

"That still leaves you, don't it? A man oughtn't to get
clean away with what you tried to do to me this night.
Ought to have somethin' to make him remember it, so's
he don't make the same mistake again."

Alfred Williams paled. Surely the man didn't intend to
shoot him with his own rifle, he wasn't that kind of man.
But such a judgment merely confirmed the rising suspicion
that he was not the brutal killer Selvy had claimed was
tracking him so relentlessly. If not, who was he? And what
of Selvy's story? Was it a complete fabrication? Why
would Dick Sanderson have participated in such a decep-
tion?

Sanderson's story had had the ring of truth, Williams remembered. And Selvy's reaction had seemed genuine. Certainly his fear had been real. Moreover, his description of
the gunman and his horse had fitted Conagher exactly, no
matter what he claimed or how ordinary he appeared now.

But that meant that he was indeed a hired killer, toying
with him . . .

At that moment Conagher's glance fell upon a large
bottle on a shelf behind the counter. He stared at it in-
quisitively. Then he went behind the counter and took the
bottle down. He turned toward Williams with a grim smile.

"Seems like there's been a lot of celebratin' in town tonight. Maybe you could use a drink."

"I . . . I don't understand."

"Little of this is good for what ails you. Seems like I remember my ma used to say that when she held my nose
and made me take a swallow."

Williams stared at the bottle like a bird transfixed by a
snake. The tall man held it toward him.

"Drink up," he said softly. "All of it."

"My God, you can't mean it! Don't you know what that would do to me?"

"You'll live," Conagher replied. "And that's the choice you got. Take your punishment and drink, or you'll swallow lead."

He gestured with the bottle impatiently, and Alfred Williams took it in a shaking hand. He looked up in a silent plea, but the steel was visible again in the tall man's eyes.

The pharmacist removed the glass stopper, shuddered, and raised the bottle of castor oil to his lips.

FOURTEEN

Dan Colgrove was angry. He was also tired, worried, and in pain—and he was holding a shotgun. All of these things made him dangerous.

He stood just inside the swinging doors of the Dust Cutter. Many of those he confronted were not thinking clearly by this time—one among them had gunned down a running cowboy within the hour simply because he was running, on the wild assumption that that meant he was the fugitive killer—but they were all silent and tame before the muzzle of the shotgun in Dan's hands.

The journey from his house to the saloon, a short walk for a normal man, had been a painful ordeal for the crippled man, and no one seeing him doubted that he would use the gun.

"Where's Willa?" he demanded. "Where's my daughter? Damn you, Selvy, if you've let anyone harm a hair of her head—"

"Take it easy, Dan," Bud Selvy said soothingly, his smile a little fixed. "You know I wouldn't let that happen."

"Then where have you got her?"

"She's safe and sound—not ten feet away from me." Selvy nodded toward the closed door of Harvey Parker's office. "She didn't much take to the idea of stayin' put, but there was so much goin' on outside I figured she was better off there, like it or not. So you can put that shotgun down, Dan, 'fore you hurt somebody with it."

Dan Colgrove frowned. The night's events had increased his dislike of Selvy, but what he said now sounded reasonable, even prudent. Willa could be hotheaded and foolish. Sometimes she needed looking after even when she didn't agree.

"I'll put it down when you turn Willa loose," he snapped. "She'll be safe enough in her own home. That killer didn't come to town lookin' for her." Or anyone else, Dan thought, remembering the quiet stranger who had spoken to him on his porch.

Selvy took a step toward him. "I don't think she should be walkin' the street right now, no more than you should. I'd take it as a favor if you was to put that shotgun away, Dan. I don't like lookin' down any man's barrel."

Selvy was still smiling, but there was a veiled command in his words, an imperiousness Dan Colgrove had heard before, although Selvy usually kept it from sounding too clearly.

Selvy liked power, Dan thought. He liked to keep other men in a position where he could squeeze them, maybe only a little to let them know what he could do if he chose to. Selvy had put Dan Colgrove in that position by giving him something he didn't have to offer—something Dan didn't want to lose.

It went back to Selvy's purchase of the disintegrating freight line after Dan's accident. Selvy had bought the line when he might have waited a little longer for the business to fail completely, as it would have with Dan on his back. What's more, he had allowed Dan Colgrove to retain a small percentage of the business, a token share, perhaps, but enough to enable Dan to put away his portion of the rising profits that came in each month. He wanted that for Willa, who didn't know about the arrangement, and he had been reluctant to risk losing it.

Selvy knew that. He had counted on it from the beginning, Dan Colgrove guessed. Had he even had it in his mind from the start to use that hold as an advantage when he came calling on Willa? In that moment it seemed likely

—and it had worked, Dan thought with anguish. It had tempered his opposition to Selvy all along. If it hadn't been for that share in the business, that hope to keep putting something away for Willa's future—something she would not have permitted had she known of it—Dan knew that he would have resisted Selvy much more strongly.

He was a clever man, Selvy. A cunning, planning man. And suddenly Dan Colgrove wanted to see him squirm a little, as Selvy had made him and others squirm.

"Put it away, Dan," Selvy said sharply.

"Maybe not." Dan Colgrove let the muzzle of the shotgun swing a little until it was centered on Selvy's chest. "Not until you open that door like I told you to."

"Now, Dan—"

"Do it!"

Selvy flushed. His round face slowly darkened, and a venomous rage replaced the deceptive twinkle in his blue eyes. "You'll regret this."

"Not half as much as you will if you don't get a move on."

It was a heady moment. Selvy didn't enjoy being faced down in front of others, and he didn't like the shotgun being turned on him. Dan Colgrove, a proud man who had never accustomed himself to being crippled and dependent on others, was human enough to relish the moment. That feeling caused him to ignore the fact that he stood only a couple of feet inside the swinging doors and to forget that most of the vigilantes were still in the street. He showed his teeth in a satisfied grin that mocked Selvy's habitual smile as the stocky man turned, glowering, toward Parker's office. Dan's attention was on Selvy as he reached for the key in the lock, and the barrel of the shotgun dipped slightly.

Without warning the swinging doors crashed inward. The edge of one door caught Dan Colgrove in the middle of his back. At the same moment Ralph Reese piled into him, one arm sweeping down to drive the barrel of the shotgun toward the floor.

The gun's blast shattered the silence of the barroom. Dan Colgrove was knocked off his feet. He skidded face down across the sawdust floor, the shotgun flying from his hands. Pain savaged his back and hip.

Turmoil erupted around him. Selvy was raging at Reese. "God damn it, you coulda got me killed!"

"Well, he missed, didn't he?" the deputy protested.

"No fault of yours!"

Bud Selvy jerked Dan roughly to his feet. "You stupid old fool!" he snapped.

His big hand slapped the older man across the face in a vicious backhand blow, bringing stinging tears to his eyes. Dan Colgrove tried to hit back, but Selvy pinned his arms, holding him as easily as if he were a bundle of rags. There was open contempt as well as anger in his cold stare.

"I said you'd regret it," Selvy said. "I promise you will."

He shoved the crippled man away. Dan stumbled and started to fall. Someone caught his arms and held him up. He was too blinded by pain and bitter despair over his helplessness to see who it was.

"Get him out of here," Selvy ordered harshly.

"What'll I do with him?" The voice of the man holding Dan Colgrove was Reese's.

"You're the deputy, ain't you? Throw him in jail!"

"You can't do that," Isiah Howarth protested.

Selvy answered him churlishly. "He threatened me, didn't he? I can bring charges and make 'em stick. A whole roomful of people saw him try to shoot me."

"You know it wasn't that way, Selvy," Howarth insisted. He looked around for support, but Ike Coolidge was silent, though visibly disturbed. Howarth wished that Tug Walsh had been there. The cattleman wouldn't have stood for knocking a crippled man around.

For a moment the dark fury in Selvy threatened to vent

itself against the newspaperman, but abruptly he checked his rage, as if sensing in time that it was racing out of control. This night had been a bad one, but it would end. He would win out—and he might need friends in the town tomorrow, reasonable and respected voices like Howarth's and Coolidge's speaking up for him. The Reception Committee shared responsibility for everything that had happened and might still lie ahead. He had to keep the committee intact and on his side.

"I don't mean him no harm," Selvy said more calmly. "Hell, he's Willa's kin. But I can't have him in the way, and he's stubborn, just like she is. He'll be safer behind bars for the rest of the night, or until this is over." He nodded to Reese. "Just make sure he's locked up and has somethin' comfortable to sleep on."

"Wait a minute," Howarth insisted. "Are you planning to keep Willa locked up all night, Selvy? Dan just wanted to make sure she was all right, and you can't hold that against him. Turn them both loose and send them home, and they won't be in the way."

"That's right," Ike Coolidge agreed, eagerly seizing a palatable solution. The near disaster of Dan Colgrove's angry intrusion, coming so soon after the shattering deaths of three people, one a woman, had horrified him. What had begun as an attempt to save the town as well as Selvy now threatened to destroy it, and the banker was anxious to avoid new complications. "Colgrove won't make any trouble if we send him home with his daughter. And it might be best if she wasn't here." He had an uncomfortably vivid memory of the body of the woman who had fallen from the Dust Cutter's balcony, her head twisted at a grotesque angle from a broken neck.

Selvy hesitated. The memory of the shotgun blast which had dug a wide furrow in the floor of the barroom close to his feet still rankled, but he knew that Howarth's suggestion was a reasonable one. He still had unfinished business with

Willa Colgrove and her father. The girl had kept him
dangling far too long to turn against him now. But here
in the Dust Cutter she was in the way. There would be
time enough for her when Rorke had been dealt with.

He turned to Dan Colgrove. "That was a damn fool stunt
to pull, Dan," he said, trying to summon up a twinkle and
a smile. Both turned sour in the face of Colgrove's hostile
glare. "You give me your word word you'll take Willa
home and stay out of this if I let you go?"

"You'll answer for all of this," the crippled man snapped.

"Every man has to answer for what he does," Selvy
answered easily. He had himself under control, and his
semblance of a grin broadened. "Even you, Dan."

The threat was pointed, but if he had expected Colgrove
to show concern he was disappointed. He sensed that he had
lost his hold over the older man—that the small share of
the freight line he had allowed Dan to keep no longer mattered.

Scowling, for he didn't like to lose anything, Selvy jerked
his head in signal to Reese. "Let her out. See they both get
home safe."

"What about my shotgun?" Dan Colgrove asked truc-
ulently.

"We'll just keep that awhile. Willa got her Winchester
back—that should keep you through the night."

When the door opened and Selvy saw the icy contempt
in Willa Colgrove's eyes, he felt a twinge of regret, oddly
sharp, for he knew instantly that he had lost something
far more important and desirable than Dan Colgrove's de-
pendence on him—something that no other victory would
replace.

He felt a sudden, savage anger. "Get back here pronto,"
he ordered Ralph Reese. "I want every man in the posse
here. It's time we found that son of a bitch Rorke and
buried him!"

FIFTEEN

Owen Conagher had been a distant witness to Dan Colgrove's angry invasion of the Dust Cutter. Conagher had broken into the rear of a small cafe up the street and across the way, searching for food to quiet the grumbling in his belly. He had found only some stale bread and dried beef, but these were enough to keep his jaws busy and stop the worst hunger pangs.

From a front window of the restaurant he had seen Dan Colgrove limping along the boardwalk. The man's hobbling gait had caught his eye, and when Colgrove reached the swinging doors of the saloon, his shock of white hair had been enough, coupled with the limp, for Conagher to identify him.

At first he had simply been puzzled. What was Dan Colgrove doing at the Dust Cutter at this hour? Why wasn't he home in bed? And why was he carrying a shotgun in so businesslike a manner?

Conagher had seen the hulking figure who followed Colgrove to the doors and stepped back quickly. Curious over what was happening, Conagher had realized too late that the big-shouldered man on the boardwalk was going to jump Colgrove from behind. When the man made his move, Conagher was on his feet, his Colt in his hand, but there was nothing he could do. He could see too little of what was occurring in the saloon.

Silence had followed the roar of the shotgun. Some minutes later the doors parted again. The hulking man who had hovered behind Dan Colgrove appeared beside him now, shoving him none too gently out of the saloon onto the boardwalk. And there was a third figure. . .

Recognition jolted Conagher.

What was the girl doing there?

An unwelcome answer came. She was Selvy's girl. She had helped to set up the ambush at the freight yard. Even on a night like this, she had wanted to be at Selvy's side.

But that didn't account for the way the big man herded the girl and her father along the boardwalk. When he had emerged from the saloon, light had glinted off something on his chest, and now Conagher realized what it was.

A badge.

The deputy. Ralph Reese by name. A member of the Reception Committee. Conagher owed him. And the way he was handling Willa and Dan Colgrove added something to the obligation.

The three figures were lost to sight in the deep shadows of the boardwalk, but from the direction of their movement Conagher guessed that the girl and her father were being escorted home. And, judging from Dan Colgrove's refusal to accept help when he stumbled, and the girl's stiff-backed bearing, they were not accepting the escort willingly.

Dan Colgrove didn't like being treated like a cripple. A proud man, Conagher thought. Not vain or aloof in his pride, but simply determined not to give in to his handicap. His daughter had the same kind of pride, the kind that revealed an inner strength of character, a core that couldn't be trampled on or bent out of shape.

Owen Conagher had been thinking of the girl, off and on, all through the night. Funny how a woman like that, whom he had seen so little of, could stick so firmly in his mind. It wasn't the way she had threatened him with her rifle, or the fact that she had surprised him by pulling the trigger of the Winchester. Other things. The supple firmness of her tall, handsome figure. Her eyes, of a strange, haunting color like violets. The way she had reluctantly heard him out when he had tried to set up a meeting with Selvy.

Owen Conagher stared after the Colgroves and the deputy. Reese was seeing them home, all right, apparently under duress. And he was alone with them.

Conagher holstered his Colt and retrieved Williams's rifle from the counter where he had placed it. He stacked the rifle near the back door of the kitchen where he could find it quickly later. For now he had to move fast, and he preferred the familiar Colt to a strange weapon. He peered outside. Satisfied that no vigilantes were near, he stepped out into the cool darkness.

He felt oddly lightheaded as he made his way cautiously through the back yards and alleys behind the main street, but he was more awake than he had been earlier, stronger and fresher, as if the little food he had eaten was already restoring him. There had been a spell when he was close to collapse from pain and weakness and fatigue, but now he seemed to have drawn on a new, deeper reserve of strength. That little nap he had had in the saloon-girl's room had probably done more good than he had realized.

He crossed the side street behind the hotel without incident and reached the end of the business district. Here he edged forward until he could peer along the street. There was activity down the line, and the doors of the Dust Cutter opened and closed as he watched. But no one was close.

Judging and accepting the risk, Conagher ran across the street.

Reaching another patch of shadow on the far side, Conagher paused. There was no outcry. No one raced toward him.

He moved on. Now the way to the Colgrove house was clear. He retraced the path toward it in his mind, determining the route the deputy would follow when he returned. And he would return shortly, Conagher reasoned. Whatever had happened in the saloon to cause the Colgroves to be ushered home this way, seemingly under guard, wouldn't keep Reese at the house. Selvy would want him back in the hunt.

Conagher, like Selvy, knew that he could not elude the vigilantes much longer. The one thing he could try to do was keep them off balance, worry them a little.

And pay his respects to the Reception Committee.

Conagher stationed himself next to an outbuilding close to the side street, which dwindled into a dusty path where it took a turn toward the Colgrove place. He had not been there long before he heard the scuff of boots in the dust. The deputy chuckled once, aloud, and muttered something to himself. When Conagher saw him, he had to resist the thrust of anger. His sharp ears caught an unsteadiness in Reese's walk, more sensed than seen in the darkness, and he heard a slurring in the deputy's muttered words.

But Reese had been steady enough when he jumped Dan Colgrove. It wouldn't do to underestimate him.

Conagher stepped from the shadow of the outbuilding as the deputy passed him. Reese whirled toward him, but Conagher rammed the muzzle of his Colt hard into the big man's side.

"Just set that Winchester down and unhitch the leg iron. No noise, no foolishness. Ain't had a chance to shoot anybody up this close all night, so don't tempt me."

Reese stiffened. For a moment the two men stood motionless while the deputy assayed his situation and realized that he was caught. Standing close, Conagher felt a nudge of surprise at Reese's size. He was almost as tall as Conagher, and there was a thick hump across his upper back and shoulders that told of heavy, powerful muscles, suggesting a brutal power. His breath was almost as strong.

But the load of whisky the deputy carried wasn't enough to make him ignore the gun pressing into his ribs. Conagher felt him relax. Reese dropped his rifle and gunbelt.

"You ain't gonna get away with this," Reese growled.

"That's to be seen. Move along now, nice and easy."

"Where you figger to git this way?"

"I had it in mind we might visit your jail."

Conagher caught the jerk of surprise his words brought, but Reese kept walking. They reached the main street and Conagher took the deputy's arm, using his own arm to cover the six-gun he held against Reese's side.

"Where's the jail?"

"Across the street there, up from the hotel."

"Take us there, like we was in harness."

Reese obeyed, although Conagher could sense the conflict in him. Help was within earshot, but its possibility had to be weighed against the fact of that gun muzzle digging into him and the belief that the man holding it was a notorious killer.

"Hey, Reese!" someone yelled.

The deputy stopped, Conagher pulling up beside him. "Tell him you'll be right along."

"Be right there," Reese called out. "Got to check out the jail."

"That's more than I said," Conagher murmured, "but it'll do."

They resumed their march toward the jail, a low adobe-brick structure a few doors east of the hotel. Conagher wondered if anyone was watching from the hotel and if anything strange was noted in the pairing. The blackness of the lowering sky was in his favor.

He noted that Reese was not sweating. Either he was too dumb to be scared, or too drunk. Conagher didn't put it down to simple courage. A man who didn't feel any fear over a six-gun held against him was a fool.

"What do you mean to do to me?" There was a trace of a whine in Reese's voice.

"That's somethin' for you to think about," Conagher said curtly, "you bein' a member of the committee set out to put me under."

There was no light in the jail. The door was unlocked,

and Conagher prodded Reese through it ahead of him. Both men had to duck under the low header. Once inside, Conagher stepped quickly away from the doorway, flattening against the wall beside it.

"You got a lamp in here somewhere?"

"Yeah."

"Light it."

He kicked the door shut. There was just enough light from the front window to enable him to make out Reese's bulky shadow. He stayed against the wall, out of line of the window, while Reese groped his way to a lantern on a hook beside the door leading to the cells in back. Conagher shifted closer to the window when the deputy picked up the lantern. There were inside shutters, heavy enough to offer protection if the jail were under siege. Conagher released them as Reese struck a match.

He was closing the shutters with one hand when Reese spun around, the lantern swinging at the end of his arm. He flung it straight at Conagher's face. Conagher threw up one arm to deflect the flying lantern. It glanced off his elbow with a painful crack. He fell backward, somehow banging the loose shutters into place over the window. Then the deputy leaped at him, head down, driving him along the wall into the bricks.

Conagher lost his Colt in that collision. He had slipped his finger from the trigger guard, not really wishing to risk a shot that would bring supporters for Reese on the run. When his right arm smacked against the bricks, the gun flew from his hand. Conagher heard it strike the floor and skid away from him toward the desk.

The two men faced each other in the darkness, their breathing audible and ragged as each waited for the other's move. It did not occur to Conagher to rail at his recklessness. What had happened had happened. It could be credited to Reese as much as to any carelessness of his own. Either he had fewer brains or more sand than Conagher had anticipated or he had been quick enough to guess that Conagher didn't have his finger on the trigger of his Colt. Conagher had thought him more than half drunk, judging by his slurred speech and unsteady walk and the whisky vapor surrounding him. Obviously Reese was used to carrying a full load. He was not as drunk as he had acted.

With a wry, fleeting smile Conagher hoped that the deputy was not cold sober. Something had to balance out his gimpy leg.

"I'm gonna break you into bitty pieces," Reese said. There was a cruel gloating in his tone. "You was supposed to be such a he-wolf, but you ain't much without your iron."

"Takes more than talk."

Reese charged. He liked to put his head down, Conagher saw. Sidestepping the rush, Conagher grabbed a shoulder and added his own strength to the momentum that sent Reese crashing head-on into the wall.

The deputy staggered back, one hand pawing blindly at his head. With a growl of rage, he charged again. Conagher tried to swing him as he had before, but this time Reese checked his plunge in time. As Conagher ducked aside, Reese banged a fist lik a big rock off his chest.

The blow knocked the breath from him. He was gulping for air when Reese rushed him again, and this time he didn't get out of the way. The deputy catapulted into him. They crashed against the desk, sprawled over it, and rolled off, tumbling to the floor. By chance, Reese landed on top. By this time he had his long arms locked around Conagher in a bear hug.

Conagher felt Reese's hands knot together at the small of his back. He had hardly begun to catch his breath after the blow to the heart. Now Reese's arms tightened, crushing the air from his lungs and bending him backward. He felt the pain begin at the base of his spine, and he knew it was going to get a lot worse in a matter of seconds.

Conagher tried to reach the deputy's face with his fists, but Reese had his head down, digging into Conagher's shoulder. There was no way Conagher could deliver an effective blow—and no way, weakened as he was by the punishment of this long night, he could break that pulverizing hold. His fists bounced off the thick hump of Reese's powerful back like rain pelting a slab of granite.

"Gonna . . . break . . . you!" Reese exulted.

Owen Conagher had no breath left to waste in a reply. His heart was thumping now, his head pounded, and he could feel dizziness threaten. A blackness deeper than the room's dark crept from the corners of his consciousness, nibbling at the fading light of reason.

Conagher's right hand beat feebly at Reese's back and fell away to the floor. And touched something cold.

He released all of his remaining breath in a sigh. For a fraction of an instant Reese's brutal grip slackened. In that moment Conagher's hand found the butt of the Colt that had skipped across the floor toward the desk.

Reese grunted in satisfaction and, as if to make sure he had finished Conagher off, increased the pressure of his hug like the last turn of the screw on a rack, bending Conagher's spine like a bow.

With all of his remaining strength, Conagher slammed the barrel of the six-gun against the back of Reese's neck.

That broke the deputy's hold. It tore a yelp of anguish from his throat, and it enabled Conagher to squirm free of the backbreaking hug.

As he struggled clear, Reese pawed at him, but now Conagher had more room to swing. He brought the long barrel of the Colt down swiftly on the top of Reese's head.

The deputy went down as if he'd been poled.

It seemed to Owen Conagher that a full minute elapsed before he could climb to his feet. By that time, Reese was on his knees, struggling to rise. Conagher waited a moment before he whipped the deputy a last time with the gun barrel. This time Reese lay still.

Conagher found the chair behind the desk and fell into it.

Minutes ticked by while he waited for the spots of light to quit dancing before his eyes and for the pain to recede from his back and chest. After a while a voice he failed to recognize as being in his mind told him that he had to move along. Someone might have heard Reese yell, or someone might become curious about his long delay inside the dark jail.

After making certain that the shutters were tightly closed over the front window, Conagher scratched a match into flame. The lantern Reese had thrown was smashed, but there was another lamp on the desk, which he lighted.

In a desk drawer he found a set of keys on a large ring. He dragged Reese by his heels into the back part of the jail, opened one of the small cells, and dumped the big deputy into it. Then he locked the cell door.

For a moment he stared down at the deputy's motionless form. Reese was breathing steadily—better than Conagher was himself.

"I was figgerin' to teach your committee a lesson," Conagher said aloud. "You sure as hell ain't makin' it easy."

He went back to the front room, blew out the lamp, and opened the door. Emerging onto the boardwalk, he turned quickly left and kept walking. At the first opening, he cut between two buildings.

When he reached a stretch of long grass at the edge of town, Conagher threw the ring of keys as far as he could into the darkness.

Turning back, he hoped the rest of the committee weren't as big and tough and mean as that deputy. *I'd like one or two more like the Englishman,* he thought, smiling wryly in spite of a split lip.

But whatever they were, he was not through with them.

Nor with Selvy.

SIXTEEN

The rain came to Bitter Creek around four o'clock that morning. Sudden gusts of wind whipped the dust along the main street into miniature spouts and set off a ghostly moaning and rattling wherever it found a loose board or wire. Then the torrent swept down upon the town with unbridled fury. Lightning lit up the huddled buildings in sudden, eerie flashes of brilliance, thunder rolled ominously overhead, and sheets of rain turned the streets into an instant sea of mud.

The fury spent itself quickly, as violent passions did, and within a half hour the worst of the storm had passed over the town to lash at the broad plain to the east. The tail end of the storm brought only a light, intermittent drizzling. Bitter Creek lay silent and dark, as if beaten down like the grasses of the prairie. There was only the sound of heavy dripping from every roof.

By that time the vigilantes had broken into demoralized, bickering fragments. Half of the recruits signed up in the Dust Cutter, with the aid of Harvey Parker's well-stocked bar, had dropped out, some too drunk to function effectively, some tiring of the fruitless sport of the hunt, others reacting to the spreading aura of fear that gripped the town. A couple of fights had broken out in the saloon among members of the posse, and Tug Walsh had angrily stopped a threatened shoot-out between two others, neither of whom was in any condition to say what their quarrel was about.

Walsh himself was dragging. He caught himself stumbling on the uneven boardwalk. He had to fight to stay awake, much less alert. He wondered what kind of a man Rorke was to keep going the way he had in spite of a bullet wound and the beating he must have taken before he put Ralph Reese down.

The deputy had been found unconscious in one of the jail cells just before the rain came. The key to the locked cell had not been found, and Reese was still inside, awake now and raging. No one wanted to smash or shoot out the lock, for there was a growing awareness of a future reckoning with Sheriff Crowder over this night's events. Tug Walsh thought it was just as well to leave Reese there. He felt little sympathy for the angry deputy. Reese had drunk too much, he had been careless, and he had been whipped. As far as Walsh was concerned, he was lucky to be alive.

The fact that he was remained a puzzle. Rorke was not acting like any hardcase Walsh had ever known.

Within the last hour, Whitey Smith had also been heard yelling piteously. He was found trussed up like a young calf, lying drenched at the edge of his corral where the pile of urine-soaked droppings forked from the stalls was deepest.

Then there was Alfred Williams . . .

Tug Walsh paused under the protection of the boardwalk near the Dust Cutter, warily studying the street before he ventured close to the light coming from the saloon. It was now the only building in town that showed any light, and that was deliberate. It was meant to tell Rorke that the hunt for him was still being directed from the Dust Cutter, and that the man he ultimately sought, Bud Selvy, was inside.

It was a baited trap, but Selvy, the bait, was no longer there.

The last meeting of the shrinking Reception Committee with Selvy had been an angry one. Tempers were short all around, and there was a new ingredient aggravating differences: fear. Ike Coolidge was so agitated that his hands wouldn't stop shaking. Isiah Howarth, a cooler head, with more sand in him than Walsh might have expected to find, was nevertheless unnerved. Selvy was not immune to the uneasiness, and Walsh himself had lost his temper . . .

"I tell you, he knows who we are," Coolidge had said nervously. "He knows every one who was there at the stables tonight, and he means to punish every one of us."

"How could he know?" Selvy demanded skeptically.

"Well . . . that girl could have told him. That Lu-Anne. He was in her room; we don't know how long."

"She couldn't identify everyone on the committee. No one could, savin' the six of you, and me and Harvey Parker."

"She could have seen us," Howarth suggested. "We met here a couple times."

"Some of you come in the back way and made sure you wasn't seen," Selvy pointed out.

"Well, *somebody* told him!" Coolidge insisted. "There's four of us down already if you count Whitey Smith. Him and Reese and Williams and Dick Sanderson. My God, he's going to get us all!"

"He didn't get Sanderson," Selvy said, no longer bothering to hide his contempt. "Dick swallowed too much smoke, is all. And not one of the four is dead—don't forget that."

"Maybe he'll get to that," Walsh said. "So far he's just havin' fun with us and trying to make the whole committee run scared. I'd say he's doin' a good job of that."

Selvy glared at him. "How'd he find out about the committee?"

"Maybe Lu-Anne told him some. He could've got the rest out of Williams. He denies it, but he'd say that anyways." Walsh grinned faintly. "He ain't talkin' much now, but my guess is he probably talked plenty when Rorke had him alone."

"You find somethin' funny about that?" Selvy asked.

"Well, that Williams is a sight to see. Every time he tries to straighten up, it hits him again. I'd guess we won't see him leave that outhouse of his before sunup, and he'll crawl out then."

"Maybe you won't laugh so much when it's your turn," Selvy said coldly.

"I'd sooner laugh a little than quake in my boots—or hide behind somebody else."

"Meanin' me?"

"Take it any way you want."

"You take chances, Walsh."

"Maybe I do."

"Oh, my God," Ike Coolidge moaned, wringing his hands.

"Stop it!" Isiah Howarth snapped. "Don't you see this is exactly what Rorke wants? He's turning us against each other, and he has half of that poor excuse for a posse jumping at their own shadows or shooting at each other— those who haven't crawled off into a hole somewhere. Are we going to let one man do that to us? Are we going to let one man whip us all?"

Tug Walsh studied the little editor, surprised by his out- burst—and not a little by the good sense behind it. He made an effort to rein in his anger. He disliked Selvy in- tensely now, and he deeply regretted having agreed to back him. But he had. And if there was one thing that Walsh found himself disliking more than Selvy, it was the idea that the fugitive gunman could outthink and outfight the entire Reception Committee and more than a score of vig- ilantes. Many of the latter might be accounted useless drifters, but there were a good many who could shoot straight, hold their whisky, and stand up in a brawl. And up to now Rorke had beaten them all.

The duel had become more personal, Walsh realized. It no longer mattered that Selvy was the man Rorke had come to Bitter Creek to kill. There must have been a dozen times during the night when Rorke could have stolen a horse and run. He had chosen to stay. He had challenged the whole town, and so far he was doing all the real laughing. Small wonder that Bud Selvy no longer had time for humor.

The cattleman let his gaze shift back to Selvy. He saw that Selvy had also clamped a lid on his hostility. If there remained something to settle between them, that would come later.

"We're not having much luck findin' Rorke," Selvy said then, breaking a tense silence. "I don't think we will. We have to force him to make a move he doesn't want to make."

"What might that be?"

Selvy rocked back in Harvey Parker's leather chair behind the desk. "He knows I'm here. If he learned all the rest of it, then he must've learned that. If we lie low, let him get to thinkin' we've called off the hunt, he'll have to come here to find me. Don't forget, he's runnin' out of time. He can't wait for daylight—he won't be able to hide then. He has to make his play before first light."

Walsh stared at Selvy skeptically. "And we just sit and wait for him?"

"Not exactly."

"I don't like it," Coolidge said. "He's too smart. Nothing we've done has fooled him. Why should this?"

"He'll come," Selvy said confidently. "He has to. He hasn't gone through all this only to come up empty. Sooner or later he has to commit himself all the way. He has to come after me."

"And you'll be here waitin' for him?" Walsh asked curiously.

This time Selvy managed a tight grin. "Now that'd be kind of foolish of me, wouldn't it?"

"Then how—"

"All that matters is that he *thinks* I'm here. He knows that's where I've been all night, whether he learned it from Lu-Anne or Williams or . . . whoever." A shadow moved in his eyes, and Tug Walsh wondered if Selvy was thinking of the Colgroves. They had been given reason enough to turn against Selvy, but Walsh doubted they would have taken the hired killer's side. Neither Dan Colgrove nor his daughter was that kind. "If he sees the posse break up, but there's still light and activity here, he has to figure I'm gonna try to sit it out here till daylight. Then he'll come."

"I dunno . . ." Walsh said slowly.

"He'll come," Selvy repeated, his tone suddenly harsh. "He's an arrogant bastard, I tell you. He thinks he can beat any man alive. And I don't have to tell you the Reception Committee hasn't given him much reason to believe otherwise."

The men in the office regarded each other in silence with varying degrees of skepticism or fear. Tug Walsh wondered how Selvy knew so much about his would-be killer. Or was he merely judging Rorke by hearsay and his conduct during this long night? He thought of the story Selvy had told the original members of the committee, enlisting their sympathy and support and leading ultimately to the ambush at the livery stables. What evidence was there that Selvy's story was true?

Admittedly Dick Sanderson had seen the gunman over in Colton. But all that proved was that Rorke was hunting Selvy. It didn't say why. There was only Selvy's word for that, and Tug Walsh realized that he had no reason to stake his life on Selvy's word about anything. He didn't trust the man . . .

But it was too late to back out. He had gone too far. Like it or not, he had to see this thing through.

But if Selvy had lied, Tug Walsh thought grimly, there would be another reckoning after this night was over . . .

Out on the boardwalk, waiting in the shadows near the Dust Cutter, Tug Walsh glanced across the street toward Selvy's Mercantile. It was dark, showing no sign of life. But Selvy was inside, waiting up there on the balcony where he could cover most of the store and at the same time overlook the street and the front of the Dust Cutter.

Selvy had slipped across the street during the height of the storm, after the meeting broke up. Several members of the posse had left the saloon with him. There was no way Rorke, even if he was somewhere close by, could have singled Selvy out or seen where he went.

After that, the rest of the plan was carried out. Harvey Parker had roused his girls and, for safety, ushered them into his upstairs banquet room. Parker was guarding the door to the room himself while one of his men stood sentry on the balcony outside. Lights still burned in the saloon. Most of the remaining members of the posse had been sent away or into hiding. A few, including Walsh, continued to patrol the street in the vicinity of the Dust Cutter. The idea was to make Rorke believe the saloon was still being protected, but no longer under as heavy a guard, reducing the odds against him. He was an arrogant man, Selvy had argued. He would weigh the odds, and when he thought them right—or as good as they would ever be—he would make his play.

It had to be soon. Walsh thought there was a faint graying along the eastern rim of the night, under that long black line of thunderheads. That pale light would spread quickly, blotting up the darkness, first from the sky, then from the land, and finally from the town of Bitter Creek.

A silent town now. Silent and fearful. How many had slept through it all? Walsh envied them. He would have

given almost anything to be able to close his eyes, to forget it all . . . anything except his pride.

The first shout jerked him out of a threatening stupor. A second or two passed before he determined its direction. Then there was another cry, and someone took it up. Fire! Fire at the bank!

The alarm prodded him fully awake. His legs started moving before his tired brain caught up. They drove him off the boardwalk into the muddy street and started him toward the bank on the run. He hadn't covered half the distance before there were at least a dozen other figures in the street, all running toward the bank. Walsh smelled smoke before he saw any flames. In the same moment he detected the glow of the fire and saw a thick pillar of smoke rising from behind the bank, he recognized a slight figure racing ahead of him, arms waving. He heard Ike Coolidge's frantic shouting with a nudge of surprise.

He wouldn't have thought anything capable of driving Coolidge into the street at this hour, in the face of his fear of the gunman's vengeance. But there was something stronger than his fear, after all. His money . . .

Coolidge stumbled onto the boardwalk in front of the bank entrance. Flames and smoke were clearly visible now. The orange light from the windows penetrated the gloom of the street, painting grotesque shadows. Tug Walsh saw Coolidge fumbling with his keys. In his trembling haste he dropped them. With a cry of despair the banker fell to his knees on the boardwalk, groping blindly.

A rifle crashed.

The sound of the gunshot broke Tug Walsh's run. A second shot came quickly, and this time Walsh heard the smack of the bullet into the boards where Ike Coolidge knelt.

The banker jumped to his feet. The men in the street were scattering, slipping and sliding in the mud. As Tug Walsh headed for cover, he cast about angrily for some sign of the sniper. The shots had seemed to come from above, probably from a rooftop somewhere along the street, but the false fronts of the buildings concealed any telltale flash of powder.

Tug Walsh dove under the overhang of the boardwalk directly across from the bank. At the same instant another bullet slapped the boards at Ike Coolidge's feet. He jumped as if he had been hit.

Then Coolidge was in the street. Another bullet tracked him, nicking one of his heels. The banker gave a shrill cry of terror. Tug Walsh realized too late what was happening. Before he could shout to Coolidge, the banker was in full flight.

No longer fearful of an unseen bullet, Tug Walsh rushed across the street to the bank. He was already suspicious of the column of smoke coming from the rear of the building, and the flames inside seemed to have diminished instead of spreading.

A quick glance through one of the front windows confirmed Walsh's hunch. There was a fire, all right, but it was contained in a barrel. It was no real threat to the bank. And Walsh guessed that the larger volume of smoke out back would be discovered to come from an old blanket or something similar.

He found the keys on the boardwalk and tossed them to another man who had approached cautiously. "Get that fire out!" Walsh barked. "It ain't much."

"What's goin' on?"

Tug Walsh didn't bother to answer. He started back along the boardwalk toward the Dust Cutter. A glance over his shoulder told him that Ike Coolidge had disappeared. He wouldn't stop running until he was a mile out of town, Walsh thought, and there was a grudging admiration in the conclusion—admiration for the man who had tricked them all again.

Rorke had accomplished two things. He had struck back

at Ike Coolidge, gaining a mocking vengeance against another member of the Reception Committee . . . and he had drawn Walsh and the other sentries away from the saloon.

But something was wrong. Selvy would not have left his cover for any reason. And Jake Hanson, who was concealed behind the bar inside the Dust Cutter, had not left his post. But there had been no sound from the saloon. Why hadn't the gunman used his diversion to make his move toward the Dust Cutter?

The truth struck hard.

Rorke hadn't been fooled. Like any cunning, hunted animal, he had sniffed danger in the elaborate trap designed to lure him. He hadn't attacked the saloon for one very good reason: He knew Selvy was no longer there.

Even as the conviction formed, Tug Walsh heard a shot. He had started across the street. Now he veered sharply left, away from the Dust Cutter and toward Selvy's Mercantile. Excitement pounded in his chest and his face was flushed. He knew that this was the moment toward which the whole night had pointed . . .

SEVENTEEN

Owen Conagher had not recognized Bud Selvy among the men who had left the saloon during the heaviest downpour of the brief storm. Even if he had been close enough and had been able to penetrate the dense curtain of rain, he didn't know Selvy by sight, had never even been given a good description of the man. But the eagerness of so many to come out into the rain had puzzled him, awakening suspicion.

In the aftermath of the storm he had watched the town grow quiet, the numbers of searching vigilantes dwindling to a few men who appeared to be concerned only with guarding the saloon, carefully but not quite carefully enough.

It was too obvious, he thought. If he had been the man they thought he was, perhaps the trap might have worked, though he doubted it. No gunfighter with Rorke's supposed reputation had earned it by being careless or easily gulled. But Rorke, if he had been there, might have felt compelled to make his attack before daylight. That was the one way in which Conagher's predicament differed completely. The day was not his enemy. He had lasted through most of the night; surely all he had to do now was survive another hour or so. Someone—Selvy for one, and perhaps others—knew the hired gunman and could identify him. Come light, Conagher would find a way to show himself without being shot out of hand. He could then establish his true identity.

Prudence argued that he should lie low until then. But

there was still a deep anger in him, a desire to punish those
who had put him through his ordeal.

Conagher was of this divided mind when he discovered
a man hiding in the small stables behind the two-story
building he had identified as Selvy's Mercantile.

The man had been there for some time—Conagher had
no way of knowing how long—and he had apparently
grown weary of his vigil, perhaps convinced that nothing
was going to happen to demand his alertness. And he had
lit a cigarette.

He was inside the stables, shielded by one of the stalls,
and he had tried to cup his match, but there was still a
brief glow of light—and it chanced that Owen Conagher
was in a position to glimpse that spark where no spark
should have been.

For some minutes he considered its meaning. It might
simply indicate that one of the posse had taken himself
out of the fight, content to rest under cover until daylight.
But wouldn't such a man have slept after so long a night?
Why keep himself awake by smoking? There was a second
possibility: the man might have been stationed there for a
purpose. He might have been sent there to watch the back
of the store.

Selvy's store.

Conagher stacked this possibility next to the elaborate
attempt to make it appear that the saloon across the way
was still the center of attention. The longer he analyzed the
twin factors, the more convinced he became that Selvy was
no longer in the Dust Cutter.

The conclusion accorded well with the picture he had
formed of Selvy during the night. Selvy was not a man who
would willingly have set himself out as bait for a trap. Such
a man wouldn't have needed a committee to do his fighting
for him . . .

Once he had convinced himself that Selvy was now hidden inside his store, Conagher couldn't stop thinking about
him. He had punished a few other men who had been party

to his ambush at the stables, but the one really responsible for that attack, for the bullet he had taken in his leg and the hours of scrabbling for his life, was Selvy.

A first gray light streaked the horizon, a sliver under the black lid of storm clouds, when Conagher crept behind the stables in back of Selvy's Mercantile. There were four stalls and a storage room. The sentry was in the front corner stall. The light from his cigarette had gone out, but Conagher heard the man shift his position, relieving the stiffness that came from sitting or lying in a confined space. Then came a weary sigh.

Hell, he's going to sleep, Conagher thought.

He considered leaving the sentry where he was, but he had to reject the idea. No matter how careful he was, he would make some noise breaking into the store. He couldn't take a chance on having someone at his back.

Silently Conagher circled the stables. There was a narrow half door at the west end of the structure—a good place for the sentry to lean out and take aim at anyone trying to break into the store from the rear.

Conagher had picked up a handful of pebbles and one large rock. He flipped a few of the pebbles toward the store. They slapped wood audibly. Conagher heard a stirring within the stables. He threw the rock. It produced a sharp, satisfying crack when it struck.

The sentry's head poked through the opening almost instantly, followed by a hand carrying a six-shooter. Conagher had pressed flat against the wall behind the half door. He took one swift step toward the sentry and brought the barrel of his Colt down in a chopping arc. Steel thunked against bone. The sentry's gun slipped from his fingers. With a soft explosion of breath, like a sigh, he crumpled to the floor of the stables.

You can sleep now, Conagher thought.

He dragged the unconscious man deeper into the stables, found a length of rope, and hog-tied him. As an afterthought, he jammed the man's own neckerchief into his mouth far enough to gag him without having him choke on it, just in case he woke up prematurely.

He had discovered no other sentries in the area. Probably it had been reasoned that too many would betray an excessive concern for the store.

Others might be waiting inside. Conagher hoped not. Selvy was the only one he wanted to meet.

But there were vigilantes in the street, and Conagher knew that he had to draw them away somehow, buying himself some time to break into the store. The idea of diverting attention with another fire occurred to him. When he thought about the bank, his mouth relaxed in a tired grin. The banker was a member of the Reception Committee . . .

Breaking into the bank, using a crowbar borrowed from Selvy's stables, was easier than he had expected. The stables also provided him with some old blankets, odd pieces of dry wood, and straw. He carried a wooden barrel into the front section of the bank. Placing it near the window, he filled it with straw and scraps of paper and a few pieces of wood. The pile would burn quickly, creating a bright flame that would last only a few minutes but would be certain to claim attention.

He used more straw, wood, and one of the blankets to start a smoke fire out back. He waited until this fire was well started before he ran back into the bank and dropped a burning torch into the barrel. The straw leaped instantly into flame. Conagher was going out the back door when the first flames licked over the top of the barrel.

He had previously staked out a position on the roof of a low building several doors east of the bank, near the cafe where he had earlier left the borrowed Manton rifle. A rope was already in place, and Conagher climbed quickly onto the roof. He was in position behind the false front of the building, Alfred Williams's beautifully balanced English rifle in his hands, when the hue and cry went up in the street.

Conagher held his fire until he saw a man run up to the front of the bank and fumble in his pocket for some keys. He had no way of identifying Ike Coolidge, the banker, but the man with the keys figured to be Coolidge. Methodically Conagher began to place shots around the banker's feet. The first two shots drove him off the boardwalk into the muddy swamp the street had become. By the fourth one, he was showing his heels.

A passing humor tugged at Conagher's mouth, but he had no time to savor the moment.

When he swung down from the roof on the rope, he dropped the last foot or so—and miscalculated. He fell at least three feet. His left leg buckled and he stumbled onto hands and knees, pain searing his leg. He was hobbling badly when he tried to run, and he was grateful that Selvy's Mercantile was close by.

As he had learned earlier, the back entrance to the store was locked. With a mild twinge of regret, Conagher swung the Manton rifle from the end of the barrel against the lock. The rifle's stock splintered on impact—but the lock broke. He dropped the ruined weapon and drew his Colt.

He was no longer concerned about the noise he was making. There was no way to break into the store without warning Selvy. He threw a shoulder into the door and it burst inward, spilling him into a long, dark room. He could smell flour and cloth and gun oil and other things, but he was hardly aware of them. All of his senses were alive to danger—to the smell of a sweaty man nearby, to the scrape of a boot, to the melting of a shadow into another shape.

Opening a door into the main store, Conagher dropped low and darted through. From somewhere above him and to his left, near the front of the building, a gun barked. A bullet thudded into the wall above Conagher's head as he dove behind some barrels.

He lay in an awkward sprawl. His leg throbbed painfully once more, and he wondered if he had started it bleeding again. His earlier fatigue was gone. There was nothing like flying lead to stir up the juices of life.

Peering upward between two barrels, he thought he saw movement along a balcony spanning the east wall. He snapped a shot toward the movement. The flash and roar of a six-shooter answered him.

Conagher looked for the stairs. He couldn't stay where he was. Selvy—he was certain that the man on the balcony had to be Selvy at last—was on the move. His first shot had come from the front of the store, the second from halfway along the east wall. When he reached the back, he would have a clear shot . . .

Conagher pulled himself up and jumped under the balcony's overhang as another bullet buzzed past his ear, an angry hornet with a deadly sting. Directly ahead were the stairs. Conagher lunged toward them.

The front door burst open with a crash. Whirling, Conagher brought his Colt level as a big man crashed through the doorway.

Then, for a fleeting instant, Conagher hesitated, delaying his shot. He took no pleasure in killing, and the man coming through the door was a stranger who had done him no particular wrong, even if he seemed bent on putting a bullet in him now. The man on the balcony, Selvy, was different. He had asked for trouble.

That moment's hesitation did him in. The man at the front of the store must have seen him moving toward the stairs as he smashed the door open, and he did not hesitate.

In the same instant in which he saw the flame leap from the other man's gun muzzle and heard the boom of the six-gun, Conagher squeezed off his own shot. But he was unaware that he had pulled the trigger or that his late shot had gone wide. There was a searing explosion in his brain. His skull seemed to shatter into slivered fragments that flew out from the center of the explosion like quills, leaving only a black, soft emptiness.

EIGHTEEN

In the cool gray light of early morning, which left pockets of darkness in the alleyways and the shadows of buildings, a crowd gathered with astonishing speed, milling around in the muddy morass of the street or stamping their boots on the boardwalk in front of Selvy's Mercantile. The word flew from each new arrival to the next: "Tug Walsh cut him down."

For a while, no one knew if the gunfighter brought down in a gun battle inside Selvy's store was dead or alive. Then someone emerged from the mercantile to shout, "They're bringin' him out! We's gonna have a hangin' party!"

Owen Conagher was only half-conscious when he first felt himself being lifted unceremoniously to his feet and hustled out of the store. The shock of cool moist air and the rough handling helped to clear his brain. He saw the faces of the crowd lift toward him, pale in that gray light. In none of those colorless faces did he find any sympathy, only hostility and anger. Voices jabbed at him. From the confused jumble of noise, a shrill cry cut through: "Here comes a rope!" In sudden panic Conagher tried to pull free.

"Easy, Rorke," someone spoke close to his ear. "No use fightin' it. Make it easy on yourself."

The speaker was a big, square, haggard man. Conagher realized that it was he who had fired the shot that luckily only creased his skull and knocked him out. If luck it was.

"Who might you be?" he mumbled.

"Name's Walsh."

"Well, I'm not Rorke."

Walsh scowled at him. Doubt flickered in his eyes, but he turned his head as someone shouted at him, and when he looked back the doubt was gone. "You was tryin' to kill Selvy."

"Damn it, he's been tryin' to put me under—or get someone to do it for him."

The tired cowman shrugged. "We knew you was comin'. No use arguin' it."

Someone was leading a horse through the crowd. Conagher recognized his own Big Red. The men holding his arms pushed him forward toward the tie rail. Conagher dug in his heels.

"Walsh, listen to me. You can prove I'm not Rorke. Wasn't there someone saw him over in Colton? Bring him out—he'll tell you I'm not the man."

"Sanderson's swallowed some smoke," Walsh answered patiently. "He's not talkin' yet, maybe never. You cost this town dear tonight, Rorke. Now you'll stretch a rope for it."

"Selvy, then. Hell, he must know his killer. Where is he? Is he still too jelly-spined to face me himself?"

The taunt got through to Walsh, causing him to hesitate. He looked around. Selvy was not on the boardwalk. Walsh spoke to someone behind him in the doorway. "Get Selvy out here."

"What are ye waitin' on, Walsh?" someone yelled from the crowd. "We wanta see him dance!"

"That's right, hang him'!' This exhortation came from a hollow-eyed man in mud-spattered town clothes. Conagher had not seen him up close or in the light before, but he had a hunch this was the banker, Ike Coolidge. "By God, if ever a man deserved to hang, he's the one."

"No hurry," Walsh said. "He's not goin' anywheres."

There was audible commotion in the store behind Conagher and Walsh. An eager murmuring broke into ragged cheers as a short, broad figure shouldered through the doorway. Tug Walsh swung Conagher around to face the man who had branded him a killer—Selvy.

The noise of the crowd died away. Conagher, who had been having trouble seeing clearly since Walsh's bullet nicked him, blinked and shook his head. As his vision cleared, he saw the stunned disbelief leap into Selvy's cold blue eyes.

The hush lengthened as the two men stared at each other. Conagher waited for Selvy to speak. He felt bitter anger, but he kept it bottled. He held nothing against the rest of the town, even Walsh, but Selvy had denied him a chance to clear himself. Something would have to be settled with Selvy—later.

"Well, how about it?" Walsh demanded. "Is this Rorke?"

The shock had faded from Selvy's eyes, to be replaced by angry dismay—and something like fear. Suddenly Conagher read Selvy's dilemma. Behind him lay the shambles of the night—fire and conflict, fear and death. The whole town had been put on the rack on his account. Now he had to say that it was all a mistake—that the man they had chased, who had turned on them and mocked them at times, who had kept them running in confusion throughout the night, was the wrong man. It was not easy for him, Conagher saw. He would never live it down. There would be no need for Conagher to exact a price for the mistake. Selvy would pay—

"He's Rorke," Selvy said. "String him up!"

Conagher exploded in rage. He tried to reach Selvy's throat with his hands, but he didn't get close. Strong arms dragged him away from Selvy—away from his only hope to save his neck. He was hauled across the tie rail with indifferent cruelty. His arms were jerked behind his back and quickly tied, the rope biting into his flesh. He felt himself being lifted into the saddle. Big Red danced uneasily, made nervous by the shouting, pushing crowd, but someone held the reins tightly, controlling the horse.

Conagher looked back wildly at Selvy. He saw the round face pale with a lingering, private horror, the mouth a bitter slash. "Damn you, Selvy!" he shouted. "You'll burn for this!"

He sensed the futility of the words even as he spoke. Then Selvy's face was lost to him. The crowd was on the move, hurrying him along the street, some men breaking into a run, others racing off to find their horses, the scene a babble of shouts and triumphant yips and pulsing excitement. Through his rage and pain, Owen Conagher heard the exultation of the mob, and he knew that no one would hear him now, that nothing he could do would slip the noose that was now draped loosely around his neck.

A tall cottonwood, one of a trio hugging the east bank of Bitter Creek near the wagon road and the wooden bridge, stood a little away from the others. The high, sturdy branch over which the rope was thrown had been used before for the same purpose. Its bark was worn and scarred where other ropes had tightened and rubbed while dying men danced in the air. The rangy chestnut was led under the branch and held in place there. Conagher felt the noose being pulled tight against his throat.

He looked up. Beyond the tightening length of rope and the high branch and the dark green foliage, the sky had lifted, brightening swiftly with the coming of the day. Conagher felt something thicken in his throat. It was a poor way to cash out, dying in another man's place for something he hadn't done, and the knowledge that he would never again witness the daily miracle of the sunrise was overwhelming.

The man called Walsh, astride a roan, rode close to Conagher. He was frowning. Little of the crowd's excitement showed in his eyes. He seemed more troubled than elated by what was about to happen.

"You got anythin' else to say, Rorke?"

"Where's Selvy?"

Walsh looked around. There was no sign of the man who had condemned Conagher to hang.

"He can't save you now."

"He's a liar," Conagher said bitterly.

Walsh stared at him for a moment. Then he turned away, scowling. "That's it, then."

Conagher looked away from him toward the town, which was slowly taking on color and definition from the light streaking the horizon. He had thought it a welcoming place. And there were good people in it, surely. There was a tall, slim girl whose image came clearly to mind. She hadn't chosen herself much of a man, Conagher thought, and the reflection hurt. Feeling this pain, Conagher smiled ruefully. Surely of all God's creatures only a man could entertain so foolish a regret at the end of his ride . . .

He knew that he had been waiting for the sharp slap across Red's rump that would make the horse bolt, jerking the support away, leaving Conagher to swing at the end of the rope. Several seconds passed before he became aware that a strange hush had fallen over the crowd. He thought at first that it was the quiet of anticipation, but it went on too long.

Conagher turned his gaze away from the town. No one was watching him.

He followed the direction of the crowd's stare.

Motionless on the far bank of Bitter Creek, a lone rider sat astride a chestnut similar in coloring to Conagher's horse, with a white apron on his forehead. The rider was a tall man dressed completely in black—long black clawhammer coat, straight-brimmed black hat, black leather boots and gunbelt and holsters. He had appeared so suddenly in his distinctive garb, as if he had risen from the ground, and he sat so still on the low bluff beyond the creek, that there was about him the quality of a specter, a ghost conjured up out of the last shadows of the night.

Conagher heard a murmuring run through the crowd gathered for his hanging. For a few moments he was being ignored, and the fact puzzled him. What could hold more interest than a hanging?

Then he understood. The stranger was tall, like him. His clothes were black; Conagher's were dark and dusty. Big Red was nearly a double for the newcomer's horse.

And Conagher had been ambushed and hunted as a hired killer, a gunman—because such a man was expected.

The stranger kneed his horse and, without haste, crossed the bridge. As he approached the hanging tree, some of the crowd parted to make a path for him. He reined in a few yards from Conagher, surveying the scene with cool interest. Briefly his gaze rested on Conagher.

"Don't mean to interrupt the proceedings," the rider said. "If one of you folks can direct me, I'll be on my way." He scanned the faces of the crowd, the deceptive casualness of his manner concealing the sharpness of his gaze. "I'm lookin' for a man lives hereabouts, I'm told. Calls hisself Selvy."

Someone swore. Another said, "It's him. By the flag, it's him!"

Tug Walsh, who sat his horse near Conagher, appeared shaken. "What might Selvy be to you?" he demanded.

The rider's gaze was cool. A faint smile touched his lips. "We was partners, once."

He seemed to notice the peculiar tension in the crowd. His eyes narrowed. They regarded Conagher speculatively. "Mind tellin' me the occasion for this rope party?"

"His name's Rorke," Walsh said, his tone thick. "Or so we was told. It's said he was hired to gun Bud Selvy down."

The man in black showed no surprise. For a moment he was silent, the faint smile still showing. Then he eased his frock coat open, displaying guns tied low at both hips. An unsheathed rifle was carried in a cavalryman's black leather sling at the side of the saddle, where it could swiftly come into play.

"Interestin'," the rider murmured. "I don't mean to spoil your fun, but there's a couple things wrong in what you say. For one, he's not Rorke. I am. For another, what's between me and Selvy is personal. There's no hiring about it."

The word flew swiftly through the crowd to those who had been unable to hear, but after that initial flurry of excited comment there was a stunned silence. Few in that crowd failed to grasp what Rorke's words meant—that Bud Selvy had lied, and that his lie had nearly caused the wrong man to be strung up. Tug Walsh's face had turned crimson, and he was not alone.

"I'll be lookin' for Selvy myself, then," Rorke said easily. "Seems like he didn't come to the party."

"Hold on." Walsh's tone was uncertain now, but he seemed compelled to speak.

Rorke had started to turn his horse. His gaze speared Walsh, quick and cold. "You made one mistake," he said. "Don't make another."

And with that he nudged his horse in the direction of the town. With overanxious haste the crowd made way for him, and he rode through the circle unmolested. Tug Walsh, staring after him, choked back his protest. He had had enough. The trick Bud Selvy had played had taken the sap out of him as surely as it had sobered the crowd come to enjoy a hanging.

"Cut me loose," Owen Conagher said harshly.

Walsh jerked around to face him.

"Maybe Rorke has a true claim against Selvy," Conagher said. "I reckon I have, too."

There were a few halfhearted objections from men who had been up all night, involved in the hunt, but their words carried no fever. Selvy's lie appalled them all. It made Conagher's actions defensible. No one would willingly hold the rope that would stretch his neck.

Tug Walsh rode close and loosened the loop. He drew a knife and sawed through the rope binding Conagher's wrists. Conagher felt the rope part and the quick, hot pain as blood rushed to his hands.

There was a bleak apology in Walsh's eyes. "If you want someone to back you up . . ."

"He's mine," Conagher said.

The cattleman nodded. He held a six-gun out toward Conagher, who saw that it was his own. Without a word he accepted the Colt and returned it to its holster.

The way through the circle of onlookers was already open for him. Ahead, beyond the dark shapes of the buildings along the main street, yellow light stained the horizon. Rorke's tall silhouette was visible at the beginning of the street, walking slowly past the livery stables where it had all begun.

Selvy would be running now, Conagher guessed, for he thought he knew the man. He must have known that his lie could only buy him a little time. He hadn't come to the hanging because he was gathering up what he wanted to take with him.

Rorke was moving into the town ahead of him, but Conagher had one great advantage. He had spent the night in Bitter Creek. He knew the town well, its streets and yards and alleys, even the places Selvy owned or had a share in. He could move more quickly than Rorke, and he could guess where Selvy might hide.

Rorke might not accept his intervention. Chasing Selvy down himself might mean a quarrel with the gunfighter, but that hazard had to be accepted. Nothing would turn Owen Conagher back. He was not a killing man, as this night had shown, but there were times, in this land where violence was common and a man was often tested to his limit, when he could not turn away from the need to fight and even to kill—if he would be a man at all.

NINETEEN

Bud Selvy had surprised the Colgroves at breakfast, both of them hollow-eyed and exhausted from a night of little rest and much anxiety. Willa tried to close the kitchen door against him, but Selvy bulled his way through before she could slam it shut. Now she watched in silent anger as Selvy drank from her own mug of coffee.

"I'm leavin' town," Selvy said.

"Good riddance, then."

There was a meanness in Selvy's stare over the lip of the mug. "I cleaned out the safe in the store, but I wasn't able to get over to the freight office. No time for it now. Your pa can do that for me soon as he can. You'll give him your key, and he knows how to open the safe there."

"I'll not lift a finger to help you," Dan Colgrove said, glowering.

"You'll do what I say if you ever want to see Willa again."

Dan Colgrove tried to reach the Winchester stacked in a corner of the kitchen behind the table. The stiffness of his hip slowed his move. Selvy stepped in swiftly, swinging the rifle he carried. The stock clubbed the older man's arm before he could seize the Winchester. The blow spilled him from his chair and wrenched from him a stifled cry of pain.

Willa Colgrove leaped at Selvy, clawing like a cat. He met her attack with a brutal backhand blow across the face. It stopped her in her tracks, stunning her. A ring on Selvy's finger caught her lip and split it.

"Try that again and it'll hurt worse."

Willa struggled for composure, blinking back involuntary tears. She looked at her father anxiously as he struggled to right his chair. When he fell onto it, white with pain, she faced Selvy again.

"Why are you running now? You got what you wanted— that man is being hanged."

"You don't understand it yet, do you?"

"No. I only know I won't go with you."

"You'll come, like it or not. And your pa'll stay and do what I tell him, 'cause he don't have no other choice."

"For God's sake, why? We're nothing to you. I'll never be a woman to you."

Bud Selvy's smile was cruel and knowing, arrogantly confident. "I can make you feel. I've done it before and I can do it again, and we both know it. What you want has little to do with it. You'll come with me because I put off pleasurin' you too damned long—and because it's the only way I can be sure that crippled has-been will do what I say."

Willa had paled as he spoke. There was a vulnerable uncertainty in her eyes, a recognition that Selvy meant what he said and that he had the ruthless strength to accomplish it.

"I still don't see why you have to run," she said without hope.

"Because that man stretching a rope down there by the creek ain't Rorke!" Selvy answered angrily. "That means Rorke is still to come, and when he does, the whole town will know I tricked them all. There'll be no living here for me, even if Rorke is cut down."

Willa stared at him with mounting horror. Conagher had spoken the truth, and Selvy was allowing him to be hanged in another's place. The callous cruelty of the deed moved her to revulsion. She had been angered by Selvy's refusal to meet Conagher at the freight office. What she felt now went deeper than anger, and she trembled with sick, helpless loathing.

And fear. Fear that Selvy could do to her what he said. Fear that he could awaken her body against her will, use her and diminish her.

"Why is Rorke hunting you—the real Rorke?" she asked dully. "It's not what you said; it must be something else."

"We was partners once," Selvy answered with a scowl.

"Then it wasn't a fight over a woman after all. And Rorke isn't a hired gunfighter."

"Oh, he's been that, and worse. But what's between him and me ain't to do with a woman. He wouldn't keep chasin' me over somethin' as ordinary as that. We was partners in a robbery. And . . ." His scowl deepened, as if he disliked being reminded of his reason for running so long, for changing identities, for always having to look over his shoulder.

"And you ran off with his money," Willa said with sudden prescience. "That's why you came here with so much money. It was stolen money bought Pa's freight line."

"It was all the same to him," Selvy answered contemptuously.

"What kind of man are you? You steal and lie and cheat . . . and you'd let another man die for what you did. Do you think I'd ever let you touch me again? I'll kill you first."

"Sayin' it is easier than doin' it. You got to have a stomach for killin'."

"I despise you!"

Selvy shrugged indifferently. "No matter. You'll do what I say. And you'll do the same, Dan. I crippled you once. I can do the same again."

There was a stunned, incredulous silence. Willa Colgrove choked back a sob. Her father half rose from his chair. The hatred in his eyes mingled with despair over his helplessness, and he fell back.

"So it was you," Dan Colgrove said woodenly. "You fixed the brake on that wagon. I should've guessed. But I never thought . . ."

"It won't be you gets hurt next time, unless you dance to my tune. It'll be her." He turned to Willa, abruptly impatient. "We talked enough. You'll have plenty of time to flap your tongue when we're alone. Right now I need your horses. Get out back and saddle up two. I won't show myself until you're ready—but I'll be watchin'."

"I won't."

Selvy's gaze was as flat and ugly and full of hidden evil as a swamp, and Willa Colgrove shivered. He said, "You want to hear that cripple beg?"

"No." The answer was a defeated whisper.

"Then move."

Owen Conagher had seen the black-clad gunman, Rorke, tie his horse to a rail along the main street and swing down. On impulse, Conagher had ridden away from the business district, climbing the knoll to the south where the schoolhouse stood. From there he had a better view of the town. And from there he saw Willa Colgrove throwing a saddle on the second of two horses standing in the small corral behind the Colgrove house.

There was consternation in Conagher's stare. Where was she riding at this hour? And with whom?

Was she running away with Selvy?

The conclusion, which seemed inescapable, struck him hard. It turned the exhilaration of his narrow escape from a rope into bleak emptiness. For a passing instant he considered leaving Selvy to his fate with Rorke. Then his mouth tightened.

He dipped behind the knoll to the south before turning Big Red eastward. A low rise concealed him from the Colgrove place until he thought he was behind it. He followed the edge of a shallow wash, muddy in the aftermath of the brief storm, and emerged near the corral where he had seen the girl.

Willa was on foot, her back toward him, standing near the back door to the house. She was holding the reins of the two freshly saddled horses. Her shoulders were slumped in an attitude of dejection—an attitude that paradoxically lifted Conagher's spirits. It was only a hunch—the girl's posture was so little to go on—but it occurred to him that she might not be going willingly with Selvy. He might have found a way to compel her to go.

Conagher had resisted all along the idea that Willa had been part of the attempted ambush at the freight yard, trusting his judgment of the girl in spite of appearances. Why shouldn't he trust that judgment now?

At that moment Bud Selvy stepped through the door, a rifle in one hand, a set of loaded saddlebags thrown over the other shoulder.

Conagher drove Big Red forward. They circled the corral in long, lunging strides, the chestnut stretching out in response to Conagher's urging. Willa Colgrove was the first to see him, and she did what Conagher had hoped. She dropped the reins of the horses she held and jumped to the side, leaving Selvy alone on the step as Conagher charged around the corral and bore down on him.

He snapped a shot too high, afraid of throwing lead too near the girl. Selvy seemed frozen in panic, his mouth gaping open. But before Conagher could draw more careful aim, the spell broke. Selvy turned and plunged back into the house.

Conagher pulled up hard. Big Red skidded to a stop as Conagher swung down. He heard Willa Colgrove cry his name: "Conagher!" It was all he needed to hear.

The blast of a rifle stopped Conagher as he ran toward the door. He broke stride, hesitated, then jumped for the step and ran into the house.

He tripped over Selvy's body and dropped to one knee.

Selvy lay in a spreading pool of blood just inside the kitchen door. Across the room Dan Colgrove stood propped up against the wall. Smoke curled from the muzzle of the Winchester in his hands.

"He made one mistake," Dan Colgrove said. "I almost made the same one."

"What's that?"

"He thought I was finished."

TWENTY

Owen Conagher waited to meet Rorke on the front porch of the Colgrove house. The gunman stopped at the bottom of the steps, looking up at him. His gaze was quick and sharp. He recognized Conagher as the man he had last seen wearing a rope.

"Selvy's dead," Conagher said.

Rorke's eyes narrowed dangerously. "You?"

"Nope. It was a man he crippled. Selvy was trying to make a run."

Rorke appeared to weigh this. He was disappointed and angry. He was a man come to the end of a very long ride, and he didn't like losing what he had come for. But he was also puzzled.

"Why?" Rorke asked softly.

Tersely Conagher explained what Selvy had done to Dan Colgrove—and what he was trying to do to the crippled man and his daughter at the end.

"Selvy had it coming," Conagher finished. "And it was a real man cut him down."

After a moment Rorke said, "I'll have to see him . . . the one you call Selvy."

Conagher nodded. "You can come to the buryin'." He paused a moment before he added, "If it means anythin' to you, he died scared."

For one fleeting instant there was satisfaction in Rorke's cold eyes, and Conagher knew the moment of danger was over.

He turned to find Willa Colgrove standing in the doorway behind him, her eyes serious. Conagher was struck once more by their vivid color, but there was a new softness in her gaze.

"Come inside," she said. "You're hurt, and you need caring for."

Conagher looked back once at the awakening town, drenched in morning light. You couldn't always judge a place by the first night, he thought. As he followed Willa into the house, he wondered if his grin was as wide and foolish as it felt.